# The Girl with the Face of the Moon

Ellis Amdur

**Colophon:**

The cover painting is "Moonlight" by Stanislaw Mislowski (1884, image copyright: public domain).

Cover Fonts are Museo Sans and Phoereus Cherokee.

For the interior, the body text is LTC Goudy and the Japanese Text is Adobe Source Sans.

Book Design and Illustrations by Ben Trissel.

# 又鬼
## 「Matagi」

# Prologue

Yes, everything dies, either too soon or at a full round of life. Either way, all is lost under the wings of death. The world spins round the sun and the sun amongst the stars, but even stars die, and who hears their cries when they flicker and dim to embers, or flare into incandescent nova, raging to what parent, what maker at their cataclysmic end?

Is the universe frozen indifference despite its cosmic fires? Is ours merely a singular existence whose answer to the question "why," is merely "why not?"

There is, however, a countervailing force to death, to meaninglessness, to entropy, to the universe as cosmic clock or cosmic quark. You know what that would be, don't you? If you live, if you breathe, you know—for there is love, the most unreasonable, unlikely, and undeniable force. We, small scraps of life, can even love the stars, as indifferent as they may be to us. Despite all the odds that there is no eternity to reward us, we love, and are at times beloved.

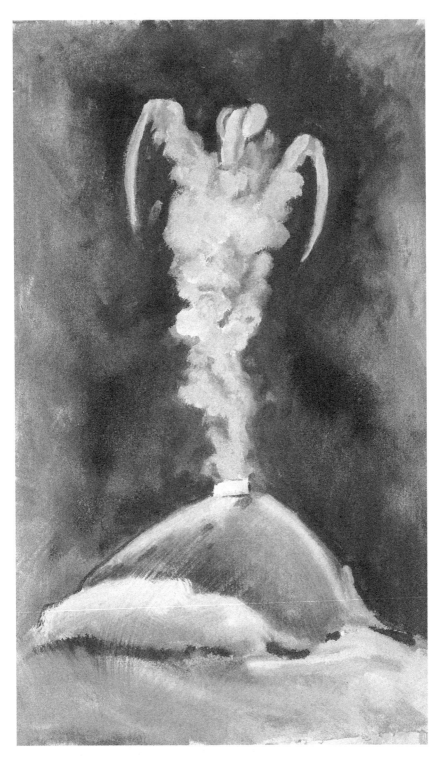

# 1

There was once a young woman, the daughter of samurai, of a family shunted off to a hillside village after a battle lost six hundred years before. I would like to make her beautiful because that seems to be required in tales such as this, but this story is true, so let us not gild this warrior's lily. She was plain. She had legs like daikon radishes, thick and straight from knee to ankle, and her face was a little flat, yet a little round, and cratered here-and-there from smallpox. The moon is a beauteous thing, glowing silver in the sky, but not a moon-faced girl. She did have a lovely mane of hair that, unbound, fell in a raven-winged waterfall down to the tops of her thighs. The villagers used to say that seen from the back she drew a gasp, but from the front only a sigh.

Samurai by lineage though her family was, they lived in the far north: eight months snow, two months thaw and two months to grow all the food one possibly could to survive the next winter-bound year. They worked the land, little different from the peasants around them, except for their overweening pride. At twenty-four, she was getting past the age that anyone would consider her in marriage, not that, un-dowered, she had much of a chance. She was strong bodied, and would have made a fine farmer's wife, but her father would rather she died than she sully the family name by mating with a peasant. Instead, she labored, her blood coursing through her body, pulsing "live – live – live," but her parents replying "alone – alone – alone." Her mother was sickly, and her brothers, two, married and away. Other than occasionally being struck in the face by her father, she had not been touched by another human being in fifteen years.

We hear of love at first sight, and can surely conceive of love at first touch. But love at first scent? He walked through the village in a late chill autumn, a spear over his shoulder, followed by a bright-eyed sand-colored dog, her tail arched over her hips. He was *matagi*, a mountain hunter, of people called 'men of winter.' He was dressed in black, with a short bearskin cloak over his shoulders, woven wicker shoes, baggy pantaloons and a large wicker hat. The matagi lived by killing: deer, monkeys, rabbits, and above all bear, whom they worshiped. Their dogs were mid-sized and utterly fearless, harassing and infuriating bears to stand and fight, until the matagi arrived to spear them to death. He was a man rare in Japan—reverent to the gods but otherwise almost entirely free. He walked with a swagger, skins and bear gall for sale in a bundle on his back.

She was drawing water at the well when he passed, and a scent, caught by a breeze, captured her in turn, a mixture of wood smoke, cold air, and something raw and violent: of stalking through valleys, a sudden rush and a dispassionate kill. He smelled of everything the village did not.

# 2

"Can I have some water, then?" He shrugged off his pack of pelts, and his dog immediately settled at his feet, ears up and alert, her eyes politely gazing off to one side. Well-muscled, with heavy shoulders, his hair coarse as boar bristles springing out in errant spikes from his leather-bound top-knot, he was a beautifully ugly man. His skull was thick, and when he grinned, cords of muscle stood out along his jaw. His teeth were startlingly white in his bronze sweaty face. He looked like he could bite through nails.

She had just pulled the bucket of water out of the well. She silently placed it on the rim, stepped back and nodded, her eyes also politely gazing off to one side. He stepped forward, took the bucket, and tucking it under his arm, squatted and carefully poured some into his cupped palm, offering it to his dog. She rose and came forward, lapping the water from his hand. Twice more he gave her water, and then she stepped back, sneezed, shook herself and settled on the ground.

Her eyes widened at this; kindness to a dog was one of the most outlandish things she had ever seen. The village had a few curs, skulking craven animals that fed off of garbage, the target of stones and kicks. Sometimes the boys would grab wooden swords, and sneaking up, would beat one of them to death—trying to break its spine with a single blow. And here, this stranger, this man who looked more like a small bear than a person, gave his animal water before he drank himself!

He set the bucket back down on the rim of the well, and taking the small long-handled cup, poured some over his hands, washing them. He took a sip and spit it off to the side. Proprieties observed, he drank: cup after cup after cup. Finally, bending over, he poured the bucket over his head and shook himself, much as his dog had done. And then, still smelling of this intoxicating otherness: of mountain passes and bears killed in close embrace, of wind through forests of cedar and mistrals howling off the peaks, he looked directly into her eyes and smiled.

She felt laughter boiling in her belly, not because anything was funny, but an outrageous joy. She was no cloistered maiden. She worked in the fields, ladling manure from buckets, and waded in water in the rice paddies with her kimono rucked up to her hips. The villagers lived half-naked for much of the year, and she'd seen them rutting in the bushes, thinking no one would notice, but not caring if anyone did. A village was a profane and boisterous place, but rules, invisible, governed every moment. You had to say the right thing, do the right thing, and this was particularly true for her, the unloved only daughter of bitter parents who clung to an empty status while living no differently than anyone else. She had no reason to laugh and never did.

In this face of a man who treated his dog better than her father treated his daughter, all she wanted to do was laugh. He was happy—not the transient emotion that passes through one after a good meal, or when one can finally rest at the end of a hard day in the fields. It was his essence.

Were he to tell of his life, such joy would be a puzzle. He risked death on regular occasions—killing bears with a socketed knife fixed to a staff, sometimes crawling into their den to fight them in the dark. His family was dead, killed in a blizzard twenty years before. Finding them frozen in one embrace, his baby sister clasped between mother and father, he knew what the bears knew when the knife found their heart, and in his agony, he never returned to his ancestral village. He was unhomed, unknown, and tied to no one. Without such ties, he could never marry. Even if he wanted to be a peasant—a fate worse than death to such a man—he would never be welcome in any village. He was always just passing through. Other than his dog, he was alone.

Women were not unknown to him. He rolled on occasion, usually widows, long untouched and unloved, who seized an opportunity when he passed through their village, or whores when he had a few extra coins. Were he somehow to find somewhere to stay, were he to father children of his own, it would mean the utter destruction of the man that he was.

Yet strange as it would seem, he was happy beyond measure. Almost every moment of his waking hours was so unspeakably alive. His life was as vivid as that of a tiger.

And now this quiet, unremarkable, moon-faced girl. He was used to women blushing and lowering their eyes, but contrary to his expectations, she turned and looked directly into his—and grinned. Then she picked up the bucket and walked off. And thus, he got a contrary view to that which the villagers were used to; the view got better as she turned away. It was her smile, however, that stayed with him, and he stood there shaking his head. True, she was plain, but her smile had another quality, as startling in its sudden appearance—blazing, white and incandescent—as the moon slipping from behind a cloud on a cold winter night.

# 3

There was no place for a stranger to sleep. There was little welcome either. 'Outsider' was not just a description; it was a fact, bone-deep. To a farmer, no one was more alien than a wanderer without roots in soil or society. Every step they took was a statement to those planted in the muck: "You could walk away if you chose." There were shadows of other hatreds as well. Cultivators of the soil encroached like a plague on land once owned only by the gods, gouging forests into fields and driving away game; in reverse, hunters and other nomads sometimes treated settled people as one more form of prey to be raided when the crops came in. So he bedded down in a grove of trees, and, looking at the full moon rolling amongst the clouds, thought about the girl.

She, awake, did more than think about him. The joy she felt remained, but now she smoldered in anguish. She burned—burned in his eyes, burned in his smile, burned in his rough hand cupping water, burned in the cords of sinew in his forearms, burned in his rank and wild smell. Would he return or would she, incandescent, burn to ashes and gutter out in the village mud?

Morning finally came, but no hunter. Each heartbeat cadenced through her flesh, pounding rage at her life, and grief at the loss of something she never owned. Hope, fear, shame, hope, more hope, hope ebbing away. She stumbled through her tasks that day, her mother's voice as nasty as a mosquito boring into her ears; her father's snarled curses tangling like clods of dirt flung into her hair. It was twilight, the villagers returning from the fields when he again appeared, walking to the well where people had gathered to wash the muck off of their hands and feet. Without a word, he spread out his pelts—bear and deer, mostly, but those of smaller animals too—and squatted beside them, quietly waiting. The villagers eyed him cautiously. Everyone already knew about him, and speculated at his conversation with their samurai's daughter, but no one had seen her smile, and there was, thus, little grounds for gossip. Knowing the vicious minds of those who live with their eyes cast down in the dirt, he did not look at her and instead waited, much like his dog beside him.

After long moments, people approached and began examining what he had to sell. Even a bit of fur could make the unbearable cold livable, and there was no end to the uses of finely cured leather. He had an easy laugh, and bargained hard, but fair. He knew how much they had, and started a little high, so they could haggle him down, and feel the winner for it. Given that the bulk of the farmers' crops were destined for the storehouses of distant feudal lords, they did not have much to spare, but he managed to sell a few pelts: three for millet, one for small dumplings made from a rough grain called *kibi*, and one for a handful of coins. The samurai's wife bought the last—a bearskin—and she ordered her daughter to pick it up. This close to the man, she began to shake and almost doubled over with pain and longing. Whatever he had, whatever he was—this was what she was not. But she did not speak. How could she? The only result would be a life heaped with shame. This would be something the villagers would never tire of, the spinster daughter of the most disliked man in their village, humiliating herself and her family by talking to someone not exactly human.

She picked up the heavy pelt, but when she returned to her parents' side, it slipped from her hands into the dust. "*Bakayaro!*" her father spat out, and cuffed her roughly in the ear, hard enough that she stumbled. By chance, she locked eyes with the hunter. He was bound here by three simple rules: no outsider had a right to interfere in the affairs of a village; no one of lower caste could interfere in the affairs of a samurai; and no man could interfere in the actions of any other in regards to his own family. Nonetheless he broke all three. Looking into her eyes, he tilted his head slightly to his left. Then he gathered up his pelts, bound them in his pack, bade the villagers good luck and goodbye, and walked off in the direction his head had inclined.

Uncharacteristically, for he had walked into the village with a firm graceful stride, he scuffed his feet as he walked away.

Night fell. The man and his dog quietly waited under a large zelkova tree, the leaves golden in the autumn chill. He ate the dumplings, and shared a little dried meat with his dog. Why did he wait? He had seen such brutality in almost every village he passed, and what could he do, anyway? Had he tried to interfere, the villagers would probably have hacked him to death with their mattocks and spades, for as much as they disliked the old samurai, he was theirs.

But still he waited. In her eyes, he saw the same look as that of a bear, he about to plunge his knife into her heart. Despair and defiance, with no escape, she still looked for a way out. So he offered it. "If that's who she is, then maybe, just maybe . . . ." And if not, then she was exactly where she belonged.

# 4

"Better death than this." She lay on her straw pallet, one hand pressed on the bruise on her cheek. The villagers hadn't even laughed when she was struck. That was the worst thing of all. Her shame was not even noticed—it was the natural order of things. The sun rose, the flowers bloomed, and she was cuffed and called names in front of the entire village.

She did not doubt for a moment what that subtle tilt of the head meant. But what if he wasn't there? "Better death than this."

She quietly rose. Her parents slept on the other side of the hearth, he breathing quietly, her mother snoring in a shallow buzz. She bound up her hair, tied straw sandals on her feet, pulled a quilted overcoat onto her shoulders, and quickly folded a second kimono in a cloth, along with a cup, a bowl, a small iron pot and some chopsticks. Moving quickly over to the cooking area, she opened an old cedar box, and with the grains whispering betrayal, she cupped out ten handfuls of millet and bundled them into a small cloth. Slipping this into the larger bundle, she tied a loop, and over her shoulder it went. Next, back to her pallet. Reaching under a corner, she retrieved a small, sheathed dagger, and thrust it into her sash. Then, carefully, she pushed aside the straw mat over the doorway and slipped outside.

Wood smoke and shit, the smells of the village. Looking upwards, though, the sky was beautiful, clouds scudding about, black cotton limned with silver, and stars, icy shards in the velvety dark. She turned back to her house and her hand reached out of its own accord, but then her expression stiffened. She could not think of a single thing that she wished to touch again. She walked between the huts, through the terraced fields, and onto the path.

She could see his footsteps in the moonlight, the scuffmarks in the trail up towards the mountains, and twice, when the trail split, a mark to indicate which direction he went.

Mile after mile she walked, deeper into the hills. Bats flew, hither and yon, catching autumn's last insects, and a nightjar called, sounding like a pebble skipping on ice.

Going uphill on a narrow switchback, she saw the man's dog, standing in the center of the path, ears up and alert, as if waiting for her.

She had not thought, not felt since she left the village. She had been pure act. Now, it all came crashing back. Her knees buckled and she almost fell. The enormity of what she had done, of how she might be received by this man, swept over her like an avalanche.

He was squatting, leaning against the trunk of a tree. Once again at the sight of her—he smiled.

# 5

Her father stormed throughout the village. He assumed that she had made some kind of liaison with a slug of a farmer, and he kicked in a few doors, rusty sword in hand. He was driven out with curses and thrown buckets, bruised in pride and body. He returned to sit on the stone beside the well, shaking—his sword impotent within its sheath. All the while, his wife searched the house, and quickly surmised what had happened. Hissing with fury—women so often hate their daughters with a passion surpassing that of men—she went outside and said, "The little bitch ran off with the bear man."

He screamed, and the villagers emerged from their huts, staring flat faced from all sides. He was about to demand that they help him drag his daughter home when he saw their faces. Behind each solemn mask was mirth. This nasty old man, no better than they in anything but an accident of birth, was laid low. Their contained laughter was so violently joyful that it promised to blow him off the side of the mountain. If he dragged her back, her existence would be a perpetual mark of his shame, and it would be the same if he killed the two of them. Either way: "Got you, old man, didn't want your precious moon-faced girl to mate with one of us? Well, that's all right. Because she ran off with a matagi, didn't she. Now she smells of bear grease and ruts in the forest."

He only had one thing left to do. "Well, guess he has two dogs now," and he and his wife turned and went back into their home.

The next day, he slipped on his wooden clogs, single toothed for the steep slope, and went to the village orchard to pick persimmons to dry for winter. His wife told him that she was ailing. She sat perhaps an hour, hands clenched so tightly that her nails drew blood. Then slowly, she got to her feet, bent almost double, and starting in the farthest corner of the house, carefully examined every surface: floor, chest and table, even the rafters over the hearth. She began to gather strands of her daughter's hair, one by one by one, laying them across her wrist. Half a day it took, and she ended up with a skein perhaps a finger's width, twice as long as her arm. She crumpled it, walked over to the hearth and blew onto the coals. She held her fist so close that the heat seared her knuckles, but just as she was about to turn it palm down, she slowly, achingly, pulled it back. Opening her hand, she caressed the snarl of hair, her fingers, calloused and hard as ivory, stroking each strand over and over. Hours passed. Finally, she carefully braided them into slender threads; then knotted them all in an intricate pattern, twined all amongst itself, inside and out, its beginning and end untraceable. It rested in her hand, light as air, heavy beyond measure, a glowing blue-black that shed absence instead of light. She opened her kimono and undergarments, three layers deep, and after placing it against her belly, bound herself tightly back into her life.

Some winter nights, she would arise and walk, unseen under the full moon, arms wrapped tightly around her middle. Were you to pass by, you would hear her weep with the sound of something tender—forever torn.

# 6

Man and now woman of winter, they wandered the far valleys where no one lived. She tore out the seams of her kimonos, then cut the rough hemp fabric. With one of his bone needles, she sewed them in pantaloons and jackets, modeled on those he wore. He taught her to hunt with snares, with poison darts, with bow-and-arrow, and with a spear. They plunged into ice-cold mountain streams, naked, hand-in-hand, screaming and laughing. They rutted like lynx, yowling under the constellations. Once he lay naked, face down in the sunlight, tawny beside a mountain brook, and over an afternoon, she traced every nerve of his body with the sharp edge of a reed. By sundown, he had involuntarily fucked himself into the soft earth, and were the mountain a woman, a child would have been born of flesh and rock.

They eventually had one of their own, a boy who seemed to smile from the inside out. He had a name, but built like both his parents, they called him *Kuma-chan*—Little Bear. They traveled through forests, cathedrals of cedars hundreds of feet in height, garbed with skirts of man-sized ferns. They denned in caves, hunting everything from fox to deer to monkeys, and clothed themselves in the fur of their kills, head to foot.

She grew to love the taste of meat, in particular boar, for which the nobility paid a premium, calling it 'mountain whale' to circumvent Buddhist strictures against taking life. (Fish didn't count, so boars became fish because the nobility said so, and that didn't make any sense at all, which is truly a noble thing in itself). She refused to eat the flesh of any animal that she had not killed herself at least once, and so she only tasted bear from the year her child was born. They had accidentally disturbed one feeding on berries—a giant of its clan—the white quarter-moon pattern on its chest gleaming in the sun as it rose to its feet in

18

warning. She grabbed the spear from her man's hand, and when he moved to stop her, she looked deep into his eyes, her wordless stare stating, "Nothing will ever hold me back again, not even you, not even death." He bowed his head in agreement and once again, she grinned, her smile a mirror of the moon on the bear. Seeing this smaller version of himself approaching, he charged. She sidestepped and gored him in the shoulder. Roaring, he whirled and finding her crouching close to the ground, rose above her. She leapt upwards, spear point first, and stabbed him in the heart. She let the weight of his falling body jam the butt of the spear in the ground. Then for the first time she heard that awful sound, for a dying bear cries like a massive child, a heartbreaking bawl of confusion and agony. She wept for him as he bled out his life. Placing her fingertips into the pooling blood, she touched them to her lips and said, "Thank you for your life. Someday, it will be my turn." She and her man performed the rituals for his soul, for the matagi see the bear as simply another tribe, half divine, half not. They concede that they are as likely to feed the bear as the bear feeds them, and thus they think they live in a just world.

# A Father

Hunters and farmers; it's always been the same. Farmers make nations and devour the earth, and the hunting clans are pushed further into the mountains.

Long ago, some became matagi, hunting not only for themselves, but also for the lords who owned them all, for the warriors who ruled them, and the peasants who lived noses down in the dirt. Others became wanderers of another sort, the sanka, the 'mountain clans,' who fished in mountain lakes and wove bamboo goods for the lowland folk.

Some, however, were squeezed in narrow valleys, surrounded on all sides by high cliffs and peaks. They had nowhere left to go. Game became scarce, and their children began to die. With no other option, they begin to kill for their own killers—and not just animals for the larder. Death requires its own prayers, and just as the matagi prayed for the bears they killed, so these people found gods of death to whom they would pray for the souls of the men and women whose lives they took.

What do you have when you take someone with specialized skills of stealth and killing, a loyalty to one's own, a hatred of outsiders, and a religious faith that prepares them for that which most men fear? A perfect spy. A natural assassin.

They flourished for a time: people of shadows, poison and blood. But Japan coalesced. A millennia of warfare finally resulted in peace, ironclad. Roads were policed and census's taken: cataloging social position, every member in each family and how much grain was cultivated in every field. Once war ended, all were taken prisoner by brush, ink and paper.

What use then, for people who did not live in ordered rows? Their villages were invaded and all of them, or at least all who could be caught, were gutted by spears or burned alive: men, women and children alike.

Only one clan remained, folding into itself, doing what no one else would do, even to survive: eating anything, no matter how foul, using their skills to cover any crime and hide in any place. Like a human black hole, they crumpled into a single group—skulking in the shadows like hyanae, other humans both prey and predators.

Centuries passed, and their skills remained intact because nothing is more incorruptible than the worship of death. Their blood, however, was not so strong. Less and less children were born, less and less of those born survived, and of those who survived, some were monstrous: flesh and bone misshapen, askew. During times of famine, they sometimes had to cull, even devour their own. They created religious rites to sanction this, deeming no one less than nine years of age to be truly human. Any sin committed on the body or mind of a little one was no sin at all as they regarded their children as animated meat, the soul only entering at the end of the eighth year, after truly fearsome rites of passage.

Their numbers ebbed and one day, they were but two: sister and brother. And brother and sister had one of their own. After they died, he was alone.

He knew no one, this one. He spoke a language, corrupt, a dialect hundreds of years old, now a jargon unique unto himself. He was sixteen when they died, victims of an avalanche. He had learned all they had to teach: he could hunt and kill a deer or even a hawk with his bare hands; he could disappear in the shadows like smoke within fog; he could enter your house and sip your wife's breath, inhaling the sweetness of the wine you'd made from last year's persimmons; he could take the water from your well, the rice from your table, the roots from your larder, and he could take your life in a thousand ways.

But there was one thing he could not do, and this was the one thing his parents said he must do—live on. They were the only People left, in a land of Them. "We must not die," they said. "You must breed."

He tried. Over the years, he must have stolen a hundred young women, some in utter quiet, leaving only an aching silence so bitter and stark that survivors stumbled when they walked through the absence where their daughters' presence should have been. Sometimes, when the mood struck him, he left carnage behind—a family hacked and slashed into gobbets of meat. He knew how to mate; not only had he seen the animals of the mountains, but he'd even mated in turn, his mother with him. He kept the girls until they irritated him with their weeping, their struggles, or their screams. Some he killed, and some he devoured. No matter what their eventual end, they never birthed him a child, because his seed was so broken that he could not even generate the monsters that in each previous generation more frequently numbered among his people's ranks.

He learned by watching both animals and men. And no fool, he eventually realized that his seed would create no child. From then on, if he stole women, it was only to rape and discard, their life span depending on what they did or didn't do, and whatever he felt at that moment. Some, on a whim, he set free, if such a word could be used in regards to what remained.

He was lean, all cord and bone, tall and lithe, and as he grew older, almost hairless. Fact and legend merged until most of the people of the north talked not only of kappa, tengu and other demons endemic to the forests and mountains, but whispered too of a Mantis who killed and raped, leaving those who survived, burned out souls flickering in women's flesh.

As he grew older, his appetite for women guttered and mostly died. But he did not leave the people of the mountains alone. Like any parent, what does one do when one cannot reproduce?

One adopts.

He tried to be a father, and truth be told, he was a little better each time. Watching through the windows, listening through floorboards, he learned lullabies, cooing, chuckling, and games; he tried to act as he saw done. But love was a mystery and so, despite his imitations, the babies withered away. He could not nurse, so he began to steal older children. One way or another, they died too. Sometimes it was a natural death: a fall, an illness, a viper, or once, a flood of centipedes during one of their strange migrations down a mountainside. But most often, they were too young, too frail, or too homesick, and so he snapped their necks and started over.

*Such a fine line: too young was too fragile; too old and the soul already coalesced within the flesh. But he so wanted to be a father. He could only try again and again.*

# 7

Nights they took their ease around a fire, sparks spinning and flaring upwards to mate with the stars. They passed through villages, selling their goods, and left as quickly as they could, the miasma of misery clutching at their throats. Sometimes, however, they would camp at the edge of the fields furthest from the village, and watch as the wind would run its fingers through the rice shoots, the acid-green paddies swirling in eddies and spirals. At night, reluctant to leave, they'd sit quietly, their son sleepy on their laps, and clouds of fireflies pulsed chartreuse. She would tell the child a story, the same story, over and over—he could never get enough of it—about the crab and the monkey: "And after the monkey killed her mother, the crab marched up the road with her helpers: the millstone, the sparrow wasp, the horseapple and the chestnut." He would convulse with giggles at the marching horseshit, and his eyes pools of wonder when the crab finally got her revenge.

When the boy was four years old, their dog ran off into the forest and was gone for a week. She returned pregnant. The matagi grumbled, because what would he do with puppies fathered by some village cur. But when she whelped, they saw to their astonishment that she must have mated with a wolf, one of the last remaining in the north. They could not care for a litter, so they regretfully killed all but one. As soon as he was weaned, the puppy slept with the boy, the two of them inseparable. He had the character of his mother, this wolf-dog, but much more than a dog, saw his family as his pack. He watched their every move, and knew at every moment exactly what to do.

# 8

Three years passed. The boy was small, but tough as mangrove root. He loved to climb and once, high up within an old cypress, he slipped and fell, his body hitting the ground so hard that his mother could feel it through her feet all the way across the forest clearing. She ran to him, screaming his name. His wolf-dog stood over him, whimpering and licking his face. He began retching, the wind knocked out of him, and then with a huge gasp, his breath caught. She pinned him down a moment, afraid he'd broken his back, but he struggled against her, reaching for her arms, bawling loudly. He held onto her for a moment, fiercely, and then wriggled free. Taking a few sobbing breaths, he suddenly stopped crying, shook himself, solemnly looked his mother deep in her eyes and said, "OW!" She was still pale with shock. He began giggling at her expression, and ran right back to the tree, rapidly climbing it once again. She yelled for him to come down, almost crying with frustration. She began climbing after him, but he thought it was a game, and simply laughed and climbed higher. The matagi returned, spear in hand, with a small boar over his shoulder, and began roaring with laughter at the sight, his son as agile as a monkey, swinging from one limb to another, and his woman, standing on a thick cross branch, shaking her fist at him and yelling threats.

She jumped to the ground and stormed in his face, telling him what had happened. He gazed up and said, "Look at him. All the while he's teasing you, look at how carefully he's climbing. Two feet and one hand, two hands and one foot. And when he has to use just his hands, watch his eyes—he studies the limb, he studies where he's going to fall and what to grab if the branch breaks. He learns. Haven't you seen? He never makes the same mistake twice." He ruefully smiled and said, "Let's just hope the next first mistake he makes doesn't kill him before he learns."

25

She glared at him and he said, "Just think what I'd be if my father hadn't given me a spear and a burning brand, and sent me into that she-bear's cave to wake her up to die, and me to be a man?"

She slugged him in the ribs hard enough to make him grunt and said, "I don't want to hear your old bear stories again." And then, after a pause, "We will be the weight on top of him, so he has to push back. He will have to fight me—and fight you—so he grows himself up to be a straight-backed man."

And with that, she turned and walked to the base of the tree, and raised her lunar face towards her grinning son, he at the moment swinging back and forth by his hands, and quietly said, "Time to come down now, Kuma-chan." He swung a little more, slower, and then stopped and began to climb down. She did not mean to stop him from climbing again; she simply wanted him to know that her influence still rose beyond the tops of the trees.

# Bones

The little one wept constantly, crying for her mother. She didn't eat. When he approached, singing rasping imitations of the lullabies he'd overheard while lurking just beyond the small circle of light that glowed around the peasants' huts, she retched in fear and wept the more, sobs of piercing terror and woe. After five days, anguished, facing yet another child who would not be his, he reached out to her and broke her neck. He roasted her on a spit. Later, he hung her finger-bones on a certain twisted pine tree on the edge of a cliff, the mountain winds stirring them and thousands more in a tinkling rattle that made him smile his rictus of joy.

Then, turning his back on the void, he opened his mouth and licked the air; tasting, smelling, searching for the scent of mother and child.

# 9

Afterwards, she wondered if she had known. It was the most magnificent autumn in memory; the mountains flaming in yellows and reds and the wind, the ferocious wind, carrying the scent of wildflowers all the way from Siberia, twined and roared through the trees. Had she known? Had she known? Had she known!? She remembered walking up a mountain path, laughing at a song the matagi was singing, and noticed both dogs, mother and son, had stopped, brows wrinkled, peering off to the side. The swirling leaves seemed to take man-shape momentarily, then shifted again and the dogs lost interest.

Some nights they would sit beside their fire, enveloped within its glow, the boy nestled in her lap asleep, and there, in the dark: a presence, a shape, a shadow.

And once she awoke dreaming of a spider hanging just above her face, with the horrifying sensation of something sipping her breath, drawing it out of her lungs as she exhaled.

And yet, it was a lovely autumn. The game was plentiful, and their son was growing. He had killed his first deer and had been trapping small game for a year, proudly contributing small furs to the family cache that he tanned himself.

Once, having met a traveler while hunting, the matagi returned with a lovely woven shawl that he had traded for his kill. She scoffed at him—what would a woman who smelled as rank as a badger do with such delicacy, but she was secretly pleased and folded it carefully away.

A lovely autumn, all yellow and red, and just like a conflagration, all was burned away.

# 10

Winter came suddenly. Caught in a blizzard, they made a dome of snow under a tree fall. They had an entrance angling upwards into a cathedral of rhododendrons, so that even if it snowed for days, the boughs would keep it from slumping into a mass. She hung a rope from one thick branch around which they built their temporary home. As the snow piled up, they shook and pulled the cord, maintaining a breathing hole. The heat from a small grease lamp soon melted the inner surface of the dome, glazing it into ice and flickering gold. Snow homes become astonishingly warm, and soon they stripped off most of their clothes, made platforms of packed snow upon which they placed layers of furs for their beds.

Over the howling winds, the matagi sang stories of tiger-gods and monkey-kings, playing the parts of all the animals and deities. They laughed, all three, until their bellies hurt, tears streaming from their eyes, their animals running from one to another, panting, happy doggish grins on their face. The boy's wolf-dog, little more than a puppy, rolled over on his back and began squirming in sheer joy.

And then in a single convulsion, he sprang to his feet, every hair erect, fangs bared and growling, looking straight above their heads. His mother, thinking he was attacking her, shied away, but then she too looked above and began her own growling.

Entering the breathing hole was a head, a narrow yellowish head, the color of old bone, with a few strands of lank hair in long matted strips. Straight down through the dome the head came, like an egg from a chicken and then it turned, with eyes small and black, like beads of hematite. It swiveled, looking at each in turn and when it saw the boy, its lips drew back in an expression for which there is no name, combining hunger and

30

lust, an avid craving for something soft and vulnerable, a desire to possess conflicting with a passion to destroy.

All moved faster than thought. The being slid through the opening, slithering down the rope in a liquid spiral, a mephitic stench emanating from his half-naked body, while the moon-faced girl threw herself over her son, and the matagi in one motion grabbed a spear, spun and pounced.

For the first time since childhood, the Mantis experienced pain at the hands of another being. Still spinning down the rope, he twisted his torso and the spear scored a gutter of flesh along his ribs, for a second white and pallid, then flowering into crimson. He continued his spin, flaring his legs outward, one hand still anchored on the rope and lit upon the hard-packed snow. The two dogs sprung together one for each ankle, trying to hamstring him the way they would attack a bear. Whipping out a flaked-stone knife from beneath his rags, he slashed the matagi dog across the throat, a spray of blood flying every which way as she whirled, gnashed her teeth and dropped. With the other hand, he grabbed the wolf-dog by the scruff of the neck, and flung him straight up towards the roof of the ice dome. But he didn't let go. Rather, he relaxed every muscle so that at full extension, the wolf-dog momentarily floated. Then clenching his body, he dropped his weight and smashed the animal to the ground. With a thump and a crackle of broken bones, it hit the stamped-snow floor, stunned and bleeding. Continuing his spin, the Mantis came face-to-face with the matagi who was thrusting again with his spear. Once again, he drew blood, the tip of his blade just nicking the Mantis' neck, but this was his undoing. Too close. The Mantis man slashed his blade across both of his eyes and stomped out the little oil lamp. Doubly dark, the only illumination pain.

"Save him! Save him! I know what this one is!" he yelled, but there was nowhere to go in the small space. The moon-faced girl drew her knife and huddled in the dark, covering her son. The matagi, standing, weeping streams of blood in the dark, became silent, listening, sniffing the air. The rank stench of the being,

31

unlike the good clean smell of sweat and smoke, filled the space like an insidious fog.

As if sitting within an ebony flower, the foul being was still.

Long moments passed. The boy was silent, his mother was still; the matagi silent, still. He knew he would die if he lunged in guesswork, and who would save his loved ones then? So he stood and he bled. Only the wolf-dog whimpered and snarled, four ribs broken, trying to crawl in the dark to savage his enemy.

The Mantis was fascinated. Never before had he encountered beings that did not act like prey; even bears and wolves were victims, nothing more. He studied their spirits: smelling their fear, their rage and their courage. After a while, however, he knew them, and he grew bored. It was time to play.

He slithered in the dark, he glided like smoke through rents in the air, and with every move, he slashed the man again. The matagi lunged, first in the direction he was cut, but then, more cannily, where he was not. Even then, he never came close. The Mantis man, after a time, put away his knife and sliding close and away, broke each tooth with a single knuckle, and tore off pieces of flesh with his nails and teeth, spitting them over the woman, who also lunged helplessly, cutting the dark. Finally, the matagi fell. Every part of his body that stuck out—fingers, toes, ears, nose, genitals, lips and tongue, and a large portion of his throat—was ripped away. Dying in the dark.

The Mantis struck flint and steel, and relit the lamp. The walls of snow and ice were painted in crimson slashes. Mother and child, covered with gobbets of flesh, screamed and screamed. The matagi, turning his half-flensed head towards them, somehow whispered, "Live," and died.

# 11

And then he turned to her. Like a heron he turned, ever so slowly moving towards her, his eyes unblinking, black lit red within, reflecting the small flame of the lamp.

Still screaming, with her child held protectively in one arm, she tried to gut him with her blade. Twining round the blade, untouched, struck her savagely in the side of her neck with his bunched fingertips and she fell, conscious, but paralyzed. He caught the screaming child in his arms, and let him fight, blending with every move, giving a little resistance here and there, testing his strength, his endurance, his spirit.

Finally, the boy, exhausted, could no longer move. And in that language all his own, the Mantis whispered, creaking like a tree root against a rock, "You boy, you boy, you be mine son." And all the while looking at the woman, staring deep into her eyes, he began licking the child, gathering up blood and flesh with his tongue, swallowing it, licking just as a cat does her kitten. He watched her eyes, she still unable to otherwise move: the anguish, the rage, the fear, and the pain, all of this food far sweeter than the blood of the man.

He dropped the boy on one of the sleeping platforms, but suddenly stiffened in pain. He'd stepped too close to the wolf-dog, silently waiting, who sank his teeth deep into his ankle. He'd be hamstrung if he moved, so he carefully twisted, almost floating in the air, held perfectly in a backwards half-loop by feet and thighs alone, like a willow branch laden with snow, arching until he could reach the beast's jaws. If he killed it, the animal might twist in a last spasm and completely rip through the tendon, so he fluttered his hands as lightly as spiders, the wolf-dog snarling, biting deeper, drooling blood and saliva. There! He found the hinge of the jaw. Pressing slowly in implacable increments, he simultaneously paralyzed the animal's ability to bite down and forced the jaws open. He was free. Not even bothering to kill it, for it could move nothing but its head, he threw it on the other sleeping platform.

He turned back to the woman. Although just beginning to recover, she was already on the attack, staring at him with a ferocity that was just the latest of the surprises this night. She could not hurt him. But he'd never seen such ferocious will.

He grabbed his knife and began to play again, slashing and cutting. Rivulets of blood streamed down her body—he'd not inflicted a mortal or even a crippling wound, just cut decorative patterns into every inch of her flesh. And still she fought. And still she stared.

He leapt up and stabbed the knife high in the snow wall, well out of reach and landing, grabbed her, all of him foul-smelling bone and whipcord flesh. He decided to do what he'd done to so many—break her spirit from the inside out. Sheathed in her flesh, the feeling was wonderful until once again, he looked in her eyes, and he knew that he couldn't touch her that way either.

He remembered fear, because he was the musical instrument of his mother half-a-century ago. Every day she played him, creating new sounds and sensations: whimpers, sobs and screams, a concerto played on the harp of his nerves. He remembered more fear during the hungry times, his father whetting his knife, considering if the need to eat outweighed the need for their blood to live. But he'd never felt fear like this; she was beyond his power. And with fear came hate.

So he clenched his fist, and struck her down, one projecting knuckle striking her precisely at a point on the side of her skull, a blood vessel breaking deep within her brain. He dropped her covered with her man's flesh and her own blood, and picked up her child, numb and still. He gently caressed the boy's hair in exactly the same way that he had seen the matagi do in the long months he'd stalked them, and knew that she knew. Then sifting around the wreck of the man on the floor, he collected all ten of the matagi's fingers. He licked them clean of blood and placed them in a small pouch at his waist. And looking deep in her eyes, he whispered, in exactly the same voice as her man, "Live," climbed up the rope with the boy and was gone.

# Birth

He shoved the child out of the air hole before him. He tried to run away through the deep snow, but it was up to his neck and he was nearly naked. The Mantis easily picked him up, and began running, zigzag, up the side of the mountain, sensing where the snow was packed and where it was feather-soft.

The boy still remembered the smell of his mother, but it was smothered by the stink of this thing, a smell like the stomach of a deer carcass, exploded in the heat of a summer day. As the being ran, the boy saw swathes of heaven, the stars cold and indifferent, limbs of trees, and an owl silently swooping by on a mission as implacable and fierce as the stinking thing that held him. The boy suddenly remembered his mother—a smile, a hug, laughter; he remembered his father, the two of them lying in the sunlight, his head bouncing on his father's belly as they laughed and laughed; he remembered his dogs, the three of them rolling in a warm furry pile, each sweet memory suddenly slashed like flesh by a blade.

The Mantis ran through the snow upwards, ever upwards. Finally, they crested a ridge, and spilling down the slope, they reached the edge of a cliff. Without pausing the Mantis jumped, landing on a ledge far below. Within the rock behind them was a cave. At the very edge was a dead pine tree, hung with thousands of finger bones that clattered against each other in the icy wind. Ignoring the boy—who first shivered and swayed, then huddled in a small bundle of himself—the Mantis made a small fire. Rummaging around in the mouth of the cave, he found a small skin bag, which he filled with snow and suspended over the flames. As the water began boiling, he grinned, eyes rolling back into his head. One by one, he held each of the matagi's fingers in the palm of his hand, licked them over and over, and then slipped them into the boiling water. He cooked them for a while, and then spilled the water onto the rocks. He took the fingers, and chewed and sucked them clean. The flesh of the last he spat in his hand. He stalked over to the boy who looked at him, wide-eyed, and grabbing his jaw, forced open his mouth and shoved the flesh deep down his throat. The boy wretched and struggled, but the Mantis merely covered his nose and mouth with the palm of his hand until he swallowed.

He went into the cave and returned with some fibrous threads, and tied each to the base of one of the fingers. The tree hung over a void, a thousand feet deep, and the Mantis, the bones hanging from a skein, casually walked along the trunk and into the branches. He moved delicately, as some of the limbs were brittle, never placing his full weight on any of them. Here and there, he found the perfect spot, and stretched, twisted, even hanging upside down, tied one of the finger bones among myriads of others. Then he'd blow a puff of air, sending them careening together, chinking and rattling. The fingers of the matagi—that once grasped a spear and drew a bow, that braided rope and cupped a breast, that cradled a newborn and cut the violet-white cord to bring him into the world—hung festooned among hundreds of years of caresses, clacking and tinkling in the winter wind.

Returning to the ledge, the Mantis kicked the remains of the fire over the edge, and picking up the boy by the hair, dragged him into the cave. He shoved together a large pile of debris: leaves and moss. The boy was pale with cold. Taking him into his arms, reeking of foul deaths long ago, now overlaid with the coppery smell of new blood, the Mantis slid deep into the moss and leaves. As their body heat began to warm them, he creaked out the versions of lullabies he'd stolen from parents before he stole their children. He did not understand why they sang, but he observed that when they did, the children calmed.

The boy did not. He fought to escape all night. The Mantis was indifferent, not even amused. He simply twisted and gripped, half-asleep, neutralizing all the boy's attempts to hurt him or escape. Finally, the child, once again, was still.

It was at this point that the Mantis very carefully, very deliberately began to hurt him. He tortured him with the exquisite skill of a violinist teasing out a note, creating a song that was an unending scream. He ushered him into a world where pain never ended, only increased, pain that varied moment to moment so that he could neither prepare for it nor blunt its effect when it came. This continued for days, the pain so awful that in the midst of it, he lost all refuge in the memory of his parents. Love had been peeled away from him. It was utterly gone.

The Mantis left him in the leaves, the cave now warmer. In the distance, he could hear other screams, those of the boy's mother spiraling up from the foothills as she careened through the forest. He smiled at the memory. "Live," he chuckled. His first joke.

In the back of the cave was a hole. It had an opening little bigger than a child's hips, and inside was a dark, noisome little compartment in the earth, well insulated with the fur of animals, poorly tanned and stinking.

He picked up the boy and shoved him in, feet first. He was wedged in, hardly able to move arms or legs, with his face six inches below the edge. Then, the Mantis took out a mortar and pestle, and proceeded to grind thorn-apple root, which bears a poison that sometimes gives an ugly death: red faced, sweating and shivering, with chaotic visions of idiocy and madness.

He inserted a finger into the evil smelling paste, and shoved it in the boy's mouth. Then he covered the hole with a blanket. Soon, the boy was screaming again, as the poisonous brew scoured his memory clean, replacing it with images of undifferentiated horror and chaos. After a number of days, the boy was soiled and filthy, his skin beginning to rot in the narrow enclosure. He was fed only a little water, crushed millet, and continuously, gobs of the vile concoction of madness. On the twenty-first day, he was fed something different, because this was the day of his new birth. This time the paste was owaraitake, big laughter mushrooms, and they deserve their name, for they impart lovely visions, all laughter and joy.

The boy writhed in the dark, trapped in his own filth, his belly heaving with laughter, and his eyes, entranced, seeing golden patterns of fractals and webs of rainbow light, patterns created by his own brain. At daybreak, the Mantis pulled off the cloth covering. The dim light burned the boy's eyes, and he closed them tightly. The Mantis bent down and pulled him out of the hole, foul-smelling and shaking, withdrawing him like a cork from a bottle. Then, embracing the child, crooning to him, he said, "My son my only one, you are mine, you are mine, I father you. We will make them weep, you and I. My beautiful son." The boy's eyes were as luminous as the North Star, empty vessels to be filled with whatever the Mantis dreamed.

# 按摩

「Anma」

# 12

The air, cold and wet, aches the bones, foot slips, whistle-warble of a cuckoo flying through the underbrush, slipping, slipping, angry, buttocks jiggling, angry, buzzing like a bee, bumbling down the mountain trail, muck and mud up to the ankles, digging the stick into the earth, a jar and twist of muscle in the shoulder as her feet slip in horseshit, HORSESHIT! That damn smell, underbrush tugging her kimono on each side of the path, room for one not for two, more horseshit, nothing meaner than a Japanese packhorse, curse the gods! Get to the bottom of the trail! They run away all the time, they kick and they bite. Have to move, have to move, don't fall, the smell of plum blossoms, sweet and rich, feet slipping, low branch whipping under the wicker hat, low branch whipping across the face, drip of blood on the cheek, smell of iron in the blood on the cheek, snot dripping out of the nose, buttocks jiggling, angry murmur of own self vibrating the bones, breathe the cold wet air through the nose, the bubbling of snot up the nostrils, a snort, a plug shooting through the air like a comet, punching a little hole in the snow, slipping again, AHHHGH! Down on the back, the wet mud plastering her wicker back-pack, the same cushioning her fall, wet mud soaking the lower portion of her kimono, so cold she pisses herself, sliding, sliding through the shit and muck and snow, bumping, slamming a rock, warding off more with her stick, jamming her head, teeth snapping together, head snaps.

Stop! What's that?

A dead body, that charnel foul smell, maybe human, maybe something on the body to use, some coin, some scraps of cloth, up on her butt, haul herself to her feet, wicker hat on, wicker pack on, straw sandals mucked up but on, edging off the trail onto the slope, mumbling and murmuring and cursing, stick out.

Remember the trail behind you, a little twist left, now right, remember where you go as you go, trees, more trees, brush and bushes, roots, falling, catching herself with her stick, the smell of death stronger and stronger, retchingly strong, tendrils of death snake up her nose, insinuating into the folds of her kimono, stinking death, babble of water about quarter mile away, smell of death, a chatter of sparrows whirl-wing away, the smell of the corpse. Thatawfuldeadthing! Croak of crows in the trees, waiting not feeding. Why aren't they already eating, it's ripe enough, isn't it? The feel of the earth, still tracking the trail behind her, up and to the left, babble of water down the slope, a little closer, there's the dead one. Oh that's foul!

A sound, a breath, another breath. Silence, another breath, another breath. Silence. Silence. Silence. A breath.

It's alive.

# 13

She jabs it with her stick. A breath. Jabs it again. A breath. Big. Not a fox, a deer? A bear? With each jab, the foul scent rises in waves. No give, not rotten. Why the smell? Gangrene? She crouches, the smell insinuating inside her, angering her, caw of crows, air cold, propping herself on her stick, strain of thighs and creak of knees, fingertips out, tracing a human torso, encrusted with something, a breast, a woman wearing scraps of cloth, tattered pantaloons, a shredded jacket, the fouldisgustingsickeningsmell! She buzzing like a bee, cursing, no purse no coin, a breath, the face round, hair long, encrusted, feels like scabs all over, the SMELL, she's covered in gore and gobs of flesh, pulse in the neck, she's alive, not dying, fingertips tracing a wounded body, slashed here and there, nothing deep, blade wounds, a tracery of thin-lipped mouths in flesh , nothing hot, no infection, the caw of crows, a small animal in the underbrush, a fox or *tanuki*.

Why the smell if it's not her wounds? Like a dog that rolled in a carcass. The sound of water cascading over rocks.

Stands up, mumbling, buzzing like a bee, bends over, twines her left hand, a meaty red mangle into the stinking crusted hair, twines it, wraps a loop around her wrist, the sound of the brook, the cold wind striking her face, a few snowflakes, ice-stars on already frozen cheeks, a heave of muscles, the buttocks clenching like a draft horse, mumbling and grumbling, she drags the woman by her hair. She goes slowly, bumping into trees with the brim of her wicker hat, slow motion caroms this way and that, the mountain path, where is the path? "I turned left, then twisted right, it's over my right shoulder," bump of the brim of the hat, the weight of the woman pulling at her shoulder, hauling with the hips, the tumbling water closer, "The path is on my left now," inexorably closer, hand a mangle, the smell foul, but the wind is in the face as is the star points of snow.

The body snags on something, "Curse the gods!" Turns around, facing the body, grabs another loop of hair, so she's closer to the scalp. She twists, left, right, left, rocking and shaking, a moan from the body, curse the thing hanging from her hand, wrenching it free, cloth of pantaloons sliding down its legs, the slow drag, bump into trees, down slope, the rush of the water over rocks, close now.

Let go of the hair, uncramp the hand, stick forward, ice on the banks, slick, a slip, ass in the water, INCANDESCENT COLD! "Curse the gods!" Edging like a crab, hand out, there's deeper water, molten ice, rushing hard, there a rock, the keen of an eagle overhead, the good clean smell of water and rock, the stinking putrid mass of woman behind. About a foot deep, the water, rocks and moss and ice on the bank. Edge backwards, edge backwards. There she is.

Heaves to her feet, rucks up her kimono, grabs the hair roughly, drags her across the roots and rocks and jabs her stick hard, there's the ice on the bank. "Stop!" Peel off her clothes, stinking clots of rags, strip her like a fruit, naked in the steely air, throw the rags in the water, and off they go downstream, grab the hair, drag her forward, jab the stick into the stream, get a good purchase, caw of crows, cold air streaming up the nostrils, snot freezing on upper lip, ARGHHH, that's cold. Drag the woman into the molten ice, spinning her out beyond into the stream, thigh deep, tethered to her wrist by her hair, water lapping over the face, sound of coughing, still unconscious, coughing molten ice, gasping for air. One hand on the staff, she lets go of the hair. Coughing, spluttering, face above the water, under the water. Bends down and roughly scrubs her body with her calloused hand, clots of scab and gore ripping off the body, breasts, face, belly and legs. Pulls the face up above the water. She's awake, gasping, about to scream. The old woman curses, rolls her on her stomach, face under water, struggling, moving slower and slower, she squats and puts a forearm under her face, raising it above the water, back arched, caw of crows, rattle of rocks falling from a deer's hooves, scrubs her back and legs, roughly combs out gore

45

and flesh from her hair with her fingers, grabs the hair, hauls her up on the river bank, drags her away from the bank, shocked by the cold, barely breathing, heart stuttering, body limp onto the feathery leaves of bamboo grass, drops her, runs her hands over her body, cleansed of gore, runs her fingertips into the lips of the wounds, tens and twenties of wounds, nothing fatal, nothing rotten, this one could live. Strips off her own kimono, feels around, there's a bush, drapes it on the bush, naked and fleshy, buttocks flexing and juggling, belly flexing and jiggling, rummages in her pack, pulls out a thick second kimono and puts it on. Tapping with her stick. Lots of leaves, "Thank the gods, but just for the leaves. Fuck you for everything else." Piles leaves head height, drags the woman onto the leaves, smell of cold air, smell of moss, the rush of the water, no more smell of death, opens her kimono, pendulous breasts and nipples puckering in the cold, buzzing like a bee, furious, mumbling, sits back on the cold leaves next to the woman, hauls her up upon her, body-to-body, lies back, wraps the kimono around them, her flesh enwombing her cold naked flesh, digs her arms deep on each side, embracing, piling leaves on top of them, more leaves more leaves, the smell of mold, the wet dead leaves, the near dead woman, she slows her breath into her belly, imagines the warmth of the sun she's never seen, she warms,

she warms, she warms herself, she warms them both, they warm, the leaves trap their warmth, their breath is slow,

their breath is slow, their breath,


their breath,


their breath.


46

# 14

A wolf-dog lies broken under a bush, the collapsed remnants of a dome of snow behind him. His tongue lolls, and he pants shallow breaths. A crow sits on a branch, waiting, occasionally opening her span of wings as if embracing the pale sunshine, chuckling softly. She has to be sure. Long hours pass, but the wolf-dog hasn't moved. The crow drops off the limb, glides down to the ground, and lollopy-hops to the wolf-dog's head. She leans over, her anthracite eyes gazing into his dull glazed orb. Other crows begin to gather, some in the trees, sitting silently, and others hopping tentatively to-and-fro. Finally, she decides, and stabs deeply towards his eye.

The wolf-dog lashes his head sideways and catches the crow between his fangs. The bird struggles, but that ceases with the crunch of his jaws. As soon as he grabs her, the entire murder of them cascades out of the trees, black roiling on black, cawing, cawing, cawing, trying to slash him with their beaks. The wolf-dog wriggles painfully backwards under the bush and into the broken cave of snow. Protected by the tangled limbs of the rhododendron, he rips his way through the feathers of its belly and eats the flesh and bone of the bird.

Broken ribs and a shattered foreleg, he could not yet walk, in fact could barely move. After his kill of the crow, he gained a little strength, something he soon lost, as the others besieged him in waves. Crows would fly off to find food, replaced by others, well-fed. Realizing that he could not attack them, they'd alight on the ground, hopping close to the skirts of the bush, cawing in rage almost in his face, or croaking and gurgling in what would sound to a human as contempt. He would have died, but for a brief thaw that melted enough snow that he had water to drink, and eventually, bared the corpse of the matagi. Frozen, he had not yet begun to rot until exposed to the air; soon, his scent, that drew whimpers deep in the wolf-dog's throat, was replaced by the smell of death. The wolf-dog spent long hours licking and mouthing his arm before rending the flesh with his teeth, and still crying deep in his throat, devoured his master's last gift, eventually gnawing and cracking his thighbones for the marrow. Within a week, there was nothing left but a few shards of bone.

Every day he gained strength, and eventually he rose to his three intact legs, the fourth curled underneath his chest. He was emaciated, weak and in pain. At twilight, the crows, as always, spiraled upwards, gathering other bands, chasing each other, calling and fighting, before flying off to their nighttime roost. A sliver of the moon lay cradled within the dark wings of the night, and the wolf-dog hobbled out from his shelter. When he moved too quickly, the ends of his splintered ribs grated together, but he soon learned to walk with the stiffness of a white-muzzled elder; his progress was slow, but he inflicted no more damage or pain upon himself. He slowly circled his lair, head close to the ground. There! Were he a sight-hound, he'd have seen crawl-marks in the earth, but there was no need. He smelled her—through the ruined flesh of her man, he caught her scent.

He had to separate himself far from the crows, hiding well enough during the day that they would not track him and slash him to death. Beyond that, achingly, perhaps a quarter mile a night, he followed the moon-faced girl.

# 15

The days warmed and so did she, lying semi-conscious in the rays of the sun, her hair swept across her face. The old woman was nearby, muttering, squatting by the warm coals of a fire, heating water and herbs in a small iron pot.

Amongst the crenulated folds of the Moongirl's brain, electric waves cascade to-and-fro, a ceaseless shower of comets inside her skull. She breathes, she dreams, she hears. Unconscious, she had been somehow aware of her body thumping and bumping across the ground, and she felt the tear of her scalp as she was dragged. Freezing water, rough hands, warm flesh and the smell of musty leaves, the mumble-snarl of her second womb, all bringing her back to life, to a world to which she did not wish to return.

Yet the heart beats. The lungs draw air, clean winter air, and the brain sparkles and hums, an ever-changing silent storm of energy and flesh. But there is an infinitesimal flaw within that inner galaxy, a tiny blood vessel torn by the impact of bone upon bone, the precise and nearly lethal impact of the Mantis' knuckle to the side of her head that first bloomed into a spot of red, then hardened into a rough and spiky pebble.

It doesn't move, this tiny meteor of blood. The energy of life sweeps within her, circulating here and there, a stream, a river, a wind-driven sky. And just as waves break onto a shoal, so too the electric tides crash and divert around this grain of corpuscles, creating eddies and whirlpools, all electric foam. All too often, a wound steals something away: a change in gait, a loss of memory, hearing or song. Sometimes, however, wounds are too much gain, not too much loss.

She stirs. Her thick veil of hair covers her face and tiny nodes of sunlight flicker through, sparkling on her closed eyes. She stretches her muscles luxuriously, and reaching up, she brushes away her lovely hair and opens her eyes.

LIGHT!!!

Coruscating shards of rainbow spears, a shrieking assault, her pupils black pools, no iris at all. The light pours in and rips through her skull. She flings up an arm, but even the slightest gap admits the ravening claws of a ferocious fire: burning, scalding sunlight.

The last thing she had seen was the wreck of her man and the face of the Mantis, her child clasped in his arms. Now seeing far too much, she sees nothing at all.

# 16

Tungsten sky and wind-blown snow, the crackle of a fire, two women crouching. One is buzzing like a bee, a drone of discontent, a rasping cascade of bitter gall. The other is still weak, her hair, two wings, wrapped tightly across her eyes and tied behind her neck. Cleansed of alien flesh after two more forced immersions in the liquid ice, she is emaciated and rocking. A tree limb snaps in the flames, and flurries of golden sparks fly amongst the snow. One woman mumbles and curses, the other screams and moans, scattershot droplets of life, falling here and there from past to further past, to future and back again.

"I had a man, a lovely man, we hunted bear, one I killed and prayed for his spirit, he shed his blood in my hands, my man and I, my bear and I, we walked the mountains, and we fucked, we fucked and fucked like deer, like tigers, like foxes and flowers, like the rocks rolling slowly in the bowels of the mountains, my father's hand was cold and dry, my mother's hard as ivory, my man and me and his dog,and his dog made a wolf, and we made a son who climbed trees to the very top and fell like a meteor, living still, a beautiful son he was. Some men you do not have to fight, you love and they love you back, we lived in the mountains, and lived with the bears, the monkey we killed with the arrow in the belly, he looked so sad, he plucked the arrow in his belly like the old woman in the village who played the *shamisen*, and then he fell screaming into the snow. We prayed to each kill, we thanked each and every one, we said prayers to the mountain *kami*, we prayed and prayed, but one kami we must have missed, and he cursed us, tore us to bits. We lived in an ice cave, glowing gold in the oil-lamp's fire, my man, a man-bear man and a man-bear boy, lovely laughing man. . . a Mantis! A gleeful torturous egg. . . hatching, spiraling down, it painted the golden ice red. We fought with will and weapons and hate and love, not enough, not enough. An ice cave, my man sliced to bits, and he covered me with him, bit by bit, he bit and bit, and all that remained of my man was in my hair and on my flesh, you took the shreds of my man away, that's all I had left, his death on me, he took My son, he took my son! Everyday is a day too late, only I and I and I and I, but I cannot, I cannot, I cannot save. . . ."

"Shut up!" The old woman's huge hand sprung out and clamped her throat, clamped the breath shut, and she rode her, knelt on her with one knee, and felt her go limp. She unclenched her hand, leaned back a bit onto the other braced leg, and waited. The moon-faced girl regained consciousness and as if nothing had happened, began to keen again, "My son, my sweet baby son, he climbed trees and killed his first bear . . ."

"Shut yourself up!" and the hand clamped down. Again, after a moment, she returned to consciousness, " . . . his first bear, a brave boy, his father's spear . . ." The hand clamped down. Over and over again, the Moongirl keened, was shut down, returned to consciousness and keened again.

The old woman muttered, she hummed like a bee, she snarled and she spat, "Shut up. You moon calf, you useless scrap, shut up." Finally, the Moongirl was silent, the first time in two days.

Were her eyes to allow it, she would have seen a face as gnarled as a root, the lips mumbling and buzzing. The hair was iron-grey and tied back severely at the nape of the neck, and the eyes were vacant, red rimmed and milky white. Once more the old woman clamped her hand tighter, but this time to raise the moon-faced girl's head a little above the ground and then to let it drop with a thump.

"Listen, you girl. You lost your son, you lost your man, a bad thing took them—that's the way of the world. Listen, you girl! My eyes were blank when I was born and I don't know who said what or who did what, but when they realized what I was, they laid me out naked on a rubbish heap, and a rag picker found me and gave me to an *anma* who happened to be passing by, blind just like me, and she carried me, starving, the two of us starving. What do you think is the lot of woman, eh? Anything good is ripped from your arms, and the good to be ripped away is rare enough. Listen, girl! An anma knows the body, knows every nerve and fiber, but men, all they think about is the cunt. This one has a bad back that won't let him sleep, and this one a shoulder, dislocated, and his family might starve if he can't get back to the fields, and that one a crick in the neck that hurts so bad that he whimpers in his sleep. You fix them, and half the time they cheat you—quite a joke to hide a coin from a blind old bitch, isn't it? And now that the neck is straight, the cock rises up, and you have to suck it or fuck it, just a blind cunt with fingers, that's what I was! Listen girl. You lost your son? You HAD your son, I've birthed seven, and I killed them with my own hands, every one! What do I want with the spawn of the men who fuck blind women? Why would I want to raise a rapist, or a girl to be raped, and how could I feed them anyway, hmmmm? How could I feed a baby, when I'm starving half the time and my breasts dry up, and the baby's cries piss off the customer, eh??? Eh!!! What do you have to say to that, girl! Seven children. By my own hand!"

"You lost your eyes? You HAD your eyes. I never had eyes, girl. You've been drinking in the sights of the world for half a lifetime. All I know is smells and sounds and human flesh, and danger at any moment that you hardly know is coming."

"I heard you, girl. I heard every word for two days running. Every word. 'Live,' he said, "Live,' the man said, the Mantis said, your jumble of words, who knows what happened. Are you just a tangle-brain? Live? I gave you life! Your life is mine, because it ended by the side of that road. So you and I, we'll live. We'll live thanks to men: pleasant voiced rapists, and hard voiced rapists, and all those men who pretend to be different. We'll live thanks to men and to all the women they own.

But your words mean nothing, even those that make sense. I don't need your voice and no one else does either, so be silent or I'll take it from you. Listen to your body when I choke you, listen what it tells you when you don't have any breath, that you want

54

life and peace and an end to pain more than you want to babble and moan after your dead. Your body wants to live. So you have no need of a voice. I will be your voice. You will be my youth."

The old woman heaved herself off of her, and as the Moongirl turned, rolling herself into a lunar curve, she put a hand on her cheek and said, "We'll live, you and I. We'll live."

# 17

Spring on the Kanto plain. Remnants of snow on the ground, the air sang clear and cold, all woven with the smell of peach and plum blossom. There had been a late season freeze, so that the roads, mud hardened, were tolerable, thronged with merchants traveling from one town to another, and farmers, no longer snowbound, going to pick up goods for the coming season. Almost unnoticed were two women, slowly walking blind, both with wicker woven hats, tapping start-stops along the edge of the road. The elder held her head rock-steady, snarling imprecations as they slowly advanced. Her eyes, under the brim of her hat, were open, a milky sheen registering nothing at all. The younger was far less sure in her movements, with a different wicker hat covering most of her face, eyes squeezed shut, with tears leaking down her broad flat cheeks. She could not wear her hair winged over her eyes because to be strange is to be feared, and then outcast or dead. She pulled her head back, swiveled to one side, or when the sun was head on, advanced with it tucked down, as if recoiling from the light. She followed the elder woman, three steps behind, tracking her by her voice.

Leaving the main road, they took narrower paths. They walked past a foul smelling jumble of lean-to's, a village of outcasts who made their living tanning the hides of the animals the Buddhists refused to touch—at least until they were turned into fine leather. Naked children gaped at them, following cautiously and then one picked up a stone and threw it, glad that for the first time in his life he'd seen something lower than himself. Soon, other children picked up stones and clumps of garbage, and with innocent cruelty darted forward, throwing with increasing accuracy. The women hunched their shoulders. Helpless, their clothes bespattered, an occasional thump of a rock on their backs, they just kept walking. The elder muttered in rage, but said nothing out loud, for with the children out of reach, there was nothing to be done. Finally a man stomped out from behind a hut, roaring in anger, and they scattered like sparrows.

A quarter mile on, a dog suddenly darted out of the underbrush beside the road, growling. The younger woman started and opened her eyes, then clamped them shut at the glare of light. The elder turned and half-raised her staff so that her right hand was at shoulder height. "G'way with you!" At the sound of her voice, the dog darted in to snap at her ankles; she kicked at it seemingly helpless, but it shied away. When she did not pursue him, he darted in again. This time, her head cocked to hear the scrabble of his claws, she suddenly cut down, striking the dog in the middle of its back, breaking its spine. The dog shrieked in pain, this cut off by the thump of a second blow to the head.

"Here!" she said, "Come here. It's dinner, but we have to go further from the village. Hard to imagine, but someone may care for the thing. If only I could do the same to the brats, but they are always out of reach." The younger woman crouched, and before picking up the animal by the scruff of the neck, ran her hands over its body quickly. She sighed in relief. Not him. Surely dead already. Better dead then than dead now.

# Raven

There is a string hanging from a limb of wood that, emerging from the rock, hangs over a void. The cliff, grey basalt, is shot through with veins of milky quartz. From the end of the string hangs a small bundle, redolent of meat grilled over an open flame.

There is a little boy, hanging by his fingers and toes to the face of the rock, climbing slowly, his body shuddering and trembling with fatigue, his eyes luminous and blank. One hand slips and he hangs over the void below, draws himself inwards and catches his fingertips onto a tiny ridge. There is blood streaming down his back. At the base of the rock face is a mantis man with an obsidian blade in his hand. He is still, the blade edged with blood, unwavering, pointing upwards.

On the stump of wood is a large raven. He's dived at the meat, but bound tightly, he can neither tear it open nor sever the string. In a few hundred feet, the boy will reach the twisted piece of wood. No food has touched his lips in many days—at each meal, he has sat absolutely still, lest he contribute a gobbet of his own flesh, watching the Mantis lick and chew. He and the raven will have a discussion about who will get to eat. Perhaps one will eat the other as well.

# 18

The village is ablaze with paper lanterns, red ones hanging from the eaves of inns, and smaller white ones, bobbing at the ends of sticks, held by people strolling up and down the lanes. Near the shrine is the high pitched wheeze of bamboo flutes, and the <Ton! Ton! Tock!> of an hour-glass shaped drum. There, coming down the lane, is a line of dancing young women, boat-like wicker hats tied to their heads, leaning back, counterbalanced by forward tilted hips, arms pointing up and forwards, repetitively poking skywards in time to the music, all accompanied by high pitched sobbing yelps: "Ei-yah, ei-sah, ei-yah, ei-sah," girls all asmile, the harvest in, the village safe enough for one more winter. And there's the base drum, the big one, carved from the bottom of a zelkova tree, fully six feet across, brawny naked men pulled it forward on a cart, chanting, sweating, two men astride, front and back, pounding the drum with sticks the size of a strong man's arm, followed by the *omikoshi*, the portable shrine, thousands of pounds, borne for a mile or more by half the village men, lurching from side to side, and someone falls, they tramp on, any blood shed is an offering to the god, they stagger on. Catching sight of the *torii* gate, a vermillion pi twenty feet high, their bodies strengthen, their feet stomp the dust, and chanting, howling, pounding, they bring the god home, back to the shrine.

For one night, the rules are off. Couples sneak away to fuck in the shadows, stealing away from husbands and wives, who very likely are sneaking away themselves. A year's worth of glances and 'accidental' brushing contact when passing in a narrow lane, smoldering desire bursts into flame this one night of the year. No one cares who fathers the babies conceived this night—those who fuck in the fields fertilize the soil for next year's crops; those who fuck in the lanes ensure the town's prosperity; and for those who somehow manage to fuck within the precincts of the shrine, amidst the pressed together bodies, kimono hiked up for a couple of thrusts, these babies are the god's own.

The young men, naked but for a strip of cloth between their legs, cram themselves in,to the small wooden shrine. More and more bodies, greasy with late summer sweat, force themselves in until some men scream in panic. More bodies cram into the god's house, so many that no one can move. Their breathing is ragged, forced and panicky. More bodies cram in. Men piss themselves and cannot move. Men faint. One skinny boy, too weak for the ritual, dies.

One man, above the noise, starts breathing loudly: suuuuuuu - - - hahhhhhhh - - - suuuuuuuuu - -hahhhhhhh - - - suuuuuuuu - - hahhhh. Soon, those near him begin to breath with him and in concentric circles, the breathing locks in, suuuuuuu - - - HAAAHHHHHHHH - - SUUUUUUU - HAHHHHHH - - SUUUUUUUUUU - - - HAAHHHHHH

They are one body now, one god. Their inhalation, thoraxes all expanding together, pushes out the creaking walls of the shrine. An exhale, and the strain on the joints of wood and flesh releases. Again and again. The shrine throbs with the breath—a huge single lung, a single beating heart.

Midnight. *Kannushi*, celebrants of the shrine, open the door that they had locked from the outside with a massive beam. They begin pulling men out, one by one. Most stagger, gasping, and fall onto the ground of the shrine, bodies steaming. They drag the dead boy off to the side. He'll be taken care of tomorrow. The celebrants bring buckets of water and ladles, and the men pour one cup over their hands, one cup over their heads, and drink one cup, no more. Then they walk off silently until they leave the precincts of the shrine, scattering in all directions like sparks from a flaming brand—some towards home, and some towards the lanterns glowing red on the street, dancing in the light breeze.

The pleasure quarter is afire. Whores lean from the second

story windows, baring their breasts, and men in clumps stagger down the street, bawling, pissing, drunk. In the entrance of one inn, two women bow low, begging entry from a brawny fat man. He nods and they enter, seemingly lost, tapping staves to find their way. "Stairs to the right!" the man yells, "Just go upstairs and see if anyone wants your services."

# 19

The fat man working the door watched the two blind women. The older one had done all the talking, and she was as polite and respectful as could be, but just as they turned away, her face slipped into something quite different. As they climbed the stairs, he heard a soft buzzing mumble, like a wasps' nest stirring. The younger one, silent, turned towards the dark corners of the street as if avoiding the light, otherwise waited as quietly as a dog for her master to tell her what to do. He shook his head. "A hard world for one without eyes. At least they aren't starving. The young one looked strong, and the old one had an ass on her as big as my own."

He turned his attention back to his job, one ear to the street, and one to the goings-on upstairs. With the moon tracing a shallow arc across the sky, the town gradually quieted. Some folks walked home to sleep, while others drowsed— propped up against the posts of the shrine or in each other's arms. The drunks in the tea houses and inns began to settle, draped like jellyfish here and there, bawling maudlin songs in each other's faces, or confiding secrets that their friends had heard a hundred times before. The whores were nestling in to sleep, or rocking one more customer, giving him that moment, that single moment where a man could be helpless and let it all go.

As the evening waned, the fat man drank steadily. He leaned himself against the lintel of the entranceway, and let his mind wander backwards to sweeter times: knowing how things would end, but worth the journey backwards, nonetheless.

"Oh gods, I shouldn't. I won't. But her cunt is as juicy and sweet as a peach. I just have to peel that fruit again. No one will ever know." He was a brawny man, with shoulders almost as wide as the entranceway to the old lord's mansion. He had taken the name Kenko, the 'Fist of Light,' just because it pissed other men off. "You have any problems with that, and I'll crush your skull like an egg." Kenko often had these conversations inside his head, particularly when he was drunk, which meant he had these conversations every day. However, no one could argue with his fist. He once knocked out a horse, smashing it between the eyes, his knuckles crashing downwards like a bag of rocks.

A fighting fat man, that's what he is—the best brawler most had ever seen, and the best fucker any woman ever felt. He can stab a rice bale with an eight-foot spear and throw it over his shoulder. His fists are bad enough, but you do not want to be hit by that belly! He will break your spine. He can stand with just the balls of his feet on a ledge, his heels hanging in space, and allow someone to charge full force into him, only to bounce off. He can lie on his back, put a single grain of rice on his belly, and pop that seed right up to the ceiling.

He had no desire to get in a fight that night, with either man or beast (or his own wife, for that matter). He'd been drinking sake since sundown, leaning against one of the cedars in the village shrine, tipping back draughts in a square cedar cup. Now he had only one thing on his mind.

He likes women, but never any particular woman. Any age, any shape, he's just a fat bumblebee gathering dew. When their men went off to work in the fields, he was sneaking in their doors. When the nights were warm, he lay in those same fields, his arms crossed behind his head, surrounded by clouds of fireflies: waiting. He wouldn't say a word, already hard, and the woman he'd already nodded to would sneak out of the house and settle herself down on him, sighing from her bones as he filled every nook and cranny of her. He loved the fucking, he loved the thrill of fear that he might get caught and he loved getting caught because that would lead to a fight with her man, which was almost as good as fucking. Everybody knew, but nobody said anything, because if they did, someone would have to do something, so when some farmer went out in the field with a few lumps on his face, everyone looked in the other direction. He loved his wife and he loved his daughters, but he not only couldn't stay home, he didn't want to stay home. Since when did a bull tup only one cow?

This one was different, though. He couldn't stay away, and that was unwise. Since the Meiji revolution, only a few years before, there were no longer any feudal lords, but here in the sticks, nothing really changed. The once-lord was still the most powerful man for miles, and he had not only wealth, but he had men—some of whom were Kenko's relatives, a crew built along the same lines as he was, which made things even more problematic, given that the lord also had a wife.

"Her cunt is as juicy – I'm repeating myself. Well, I want to bury my head again between those thighs and seal my lips on that juicy . . .shhhhh, I have to be quiet now." The back gate was open. He sidled inside, and stumbled over a bucket that had been left near the stables. "Careful, careful. Yes, there she was, beckoning from her room. These samurai never slept in the same room as their wives, they had their own quarters, and he's a once a month man anyway, which is why your humble servant has been requested to come calling." However, this was too risky. She couldn't publicly leave the house, so he had to somehow sneak in, do the deed, and rock her into absolutely silent screams of ecstasy. "I'm just too damn good and too damn big. How can a woman keep silent with me?" She usually moaned and he would stop, and she would laugh and he would laugh and they'd start again, and she'd start moaning, and on and on.

Up the veranda. Bend down and pick up the sandals. Can't leave them outside where anyone can see! There she is. Oh gods, there she is. There IT is! What a sight. A mouth of ruby and coral, garlanded in black feathers. Oh gods, I'm not playing around this time." He hitched up his kimono, tucked the back into his sash, and pulling his loincloth aside, hauled out his prick. She smiled and he more or less dived on top of her. Too drunk. He smashed his head completely through one of the *shoji*, and yanking it back, scraped grooves in his cheeks with the broken wood. The next thing he knew, the lord was storming into the room, short sword in hand.

"Husband, save me! This man is raping me!" In the dim light, he did not recognize Kenko. If he had, perhaps the lord would have been more cautious, because although he was like a dog around women in heat, Kenko was no clown, even drunk. The lord slashed out with his sword, and Kenko dropped down low, then dived underneath the blade in an undulating swoop that one would think impossible for such a bulky man. Once inside, he gripped the other man's belt and catching his leg with his own, smashed him to the tatami mats, all of his body weight impacting onto the lord's ribs, three of which promptly broke. Kenko sat on his chest, the ends of the broken bones grinding together. With one foot, he pinned the lord's sword arm and then smashed him right between the eyes with his horse-stunning fist.

He heaved himself off the unconscious man, and turned to find the wife holding a dagger to her own throat. "You idiot, we are dead. I may as well kill myself now."

Kenko shook the sake from his brain. Sick to his stomach, he realized his life was over. "Well, maybe. Yes. No! NO! NO! Not if I disappear like a criminal. I think your husband will say nothing. I can't stay. No one would believe that I would rape a woman. I don't have to."

She made a disgusted face. "If only you were half as smart as your prick is long." She tightened her arms to cut her own throat, saying, " I cannot believe that those are my last words!"

"No! No! Seriously. Listen. I'll leave. I'll never come back. People will wonder what happened, but if you won't say, he won't say."

She stared at him, then resheathed her blade. "Never come back. Because if you do, I promise you, I will cut it off myself."

Kenko slipped on his sandals, and just before jumping off the veranda, he heard the man moaning himself back to consciousness, and the woman, saying, "Wake up, husband. He's gone. Are you all right? May the gods preserve us! You're hurt. Don't move. Lie there. Yes, lie still. I'll get help. Praise the gods you saved me. You are so brave. You scared him away. No, I don't know who he was, except he smelled like he'd been on the road a long time. Maybe one of those *ronin*, those out of work oath-breakers that are robbing good people and molesting women. Husband! Thank the gods you came when you did. You saved me!"

Kenko arrived back at his home. His wife, bitterly resigned to his outings, was fast asleep as were his two daughters. He bundled up some clothing and a short sword, and laid a sprig of *yamabuki*, just in bloom, beside his wife's futon.

He bent over his daughters tenderly, kissed each on the forehead and whispered, "Don't marry someone like me."

Fat man drowsing in a whorehouse door.

# 20

A bony merchant, a dealer in candies, lies face down on a futon. "Half price for your apprentice, right? And if I don't like it, I don't pay a *sen*, yeah?" The older woman agrees, and the younger one places her hands on the man's back and begins massaging. The old woman listens to the sound of her hands on his skin, places hers on the Moongirl's, and shapes the movements, the grip, and the pressure. She works down his hips, separating the fibers of the calves and then kneels on his feet, rotating her hips so that her kneecaps roll and rock. She feels for lymph glands along the creases of the joints and under the ribs. He moans and says, "You are good, anma. If I hadn't just fucked my brains out with that whore who just left, I'd finish with that, but I'm jelly."

The older woman stiffens at that, but perceiving no intent behind the words, just the compliment of a typical man who thinks his penis is a treasure any woman would crave, she busies herself within her pack and asks, "A dry cough, right? And aching joints every morning?"

"Yeah, that's right."

She sidles to the sliding door of the room and calls down the hallway, asking for hot water "for the master." A maid returns with a tray, a cup and a small kettle, with a texture of small raised nubs like iron Braille. The old woman begins pulling small bundles of bound leaves from her pack; each one tied with a different knot and folded in a different shape. She feels each one quickly, and decides on three, which she opens dexterously with the fingers of one hand, pouring a minute portion of the dried herbs into a cup, folding and retying each bundle in its unique pattern, then pouring water over the herbs.

"*Dannasama*. Drink this. It'll taste bad, but your complaints will be gone in a week."

The man drank the cup down in a gulp, made a bitter face, and lay back on the futon.

All in all, it was a good night; the Moongirl was getting skilled enough that the customers had no complaints, and this night, at least, no one made any attempt to use her and . . . suddenly, there was shouting outside the room.

"Hey Kenko! Trouble!" The fat man awoke, finding himself back amidst the sweat and booze and noise. He heaved himself onto his feet, and stomped into the building. He could hear screams of two of the whores, coming closer as they ran down the hallway in his direction, the crashing of a table as it was thrown through one of the shoji, and the bellowing of a drunken man.

There he was, about fifty years old. He had a sword-cane unsheathed in his hand, and he was red-eyed with drink and rage. "Come back, you bitches. You don't want to be fucked in the ass? You're whores. What say do you have in it?" He threw up on the polished floor. Kenko moved closer, and quietly said, "Dannasama. I apologize that the service here left something to be desired. There are specialty establishments for those of unusual tastes. I'll be happy to accompany you to one of them, just down the street."

"Fuck off, fat man. Do you have any idea who I am? I am Aizawa Umata Tsunezaemon. I served with Kondo Isamu himself, and fought in the Shinsengumi! Bring those whores back to me and hold them down. Unless you want my blade shoved up in your guts."

Kenko sighed. "I can't believe it. Modern times. We have a steam locomotive in Tokyo, I hear. We have our national army buying cannons from the Prussians. And we have assholes reciting their lineage like it's the 12th century. See, there are two kinds of assholes. There are assholes who lie about such things, and there are assholes who are telling the truth and shame a proud organization for whom they once fought, but the one

68

thing these two types of assholes do have in common is that they are both full of rancid shit."

Well, that sobered him up! He didn't yell; he didn't deny it. He just raised his sword blade above his head, and started walking purposely forward, intending to cut Kenko in two. When he reached four steps away, Kenko threw a short double-weighted chain, which he'd held unseen in his hand. The chunks of iron at the ends of the chain smashed the man right in the face, cracking his cheekbone and breaking his nose. Blinded and in pain, he cut down where he thought Kenko would be. He wasn't. As Kenko slipped past the descending blade, Aizawa attempted to whip it sideways. Kenko had stepped too close, however, and as Aizawa's elbow struck his massive torso, he wrapped his arm around it like a grapevine. With the other hand, he disarmed him, throwing the swordblade aside. His elbow locked, unable to move without dislocating the joint, Aizawa snarled, "Let me go. You can't damage the customers, or your boss will have to close down. You think this is over. I'll be back, when those bitches least expect it. How's your business going to be when all your whores have their tits cut off?"

"I so wish you hadn't said that, danna. Otherwise, I would have been happy to walk you home. And on the way, we would have stopped somewhere for a drink or two or three, and we would have laughed, and told each other wonderful lies about the fucking and the fighting we've never done. But I like women. That's why I like working here. I don't like men who like hurting women. So I guess I'm going to have to hurt you, so you can't do that anymore."

At which point he dismantled him. He stomped the knee that the man had braced to fight off the arm lock, snapping all the ligaments, and as the man buckled, he popped his belly forward and ripped the elbow apart. He let him drop to the ground, screaming in a high-pitched wheeze. Then, bending over, he clenched his fist and chopped down, like cutting wood, once, twice, breaking his collar bone on each side. The screaming irri-

69

tated him, so he cuffed him upside the temple and knocked him unconscious. He picked him up and slung him over his shoulder, past the gaping patrons and gasping whores. Carrying him outside, he dumped him in a ditch, face-up so he wouldn't drown in the muck. Stomping back to the brothel, he walked up to the owner, who was sadly shaking his head.

"I know, I know. He's got friends. He knows people. Settle up with my wages. I'll be gone before they get here. First, his friends have to notice he's missing, and then they have to go all the way to Odawara to talk to the magistrate. And my name's not Saito—you probably knew that." The whoremonger, an unhappy man in the best of circumstances, stared counting out coins. When he stopped, Kenko raised an eyebrow.

"Damages to the establishment. And I'm going to have to pay off the magistrate. What a mess."

Kenko shook his head. He went to his room, gathered his things and strode out, giving numerous whores one last squeeze or grab-ass on the way. Sighing, he walked down the street, weaving through knots of drunks, hugging, fighting, bawling out songs or peeling off to piss at the side of the road. The red lanterns shed a warm glow, and he could hear a jumble of laughter, the twang of shamisen music, singing, eating, fucking. The sound was a comfort. He could always find a home such as this. One was the same as the other. The whores genuinely liked him just as he liked them. They were warm and so was he. He was on the far side of sixty, just a rolling stone, with no reason to stop, just a need to occasionally change direction.

# 21

They came at dawn. Not the police. They began pounding on the door with clubs, and when no one answered, kicked it down, storming through the building, beating patrons and whores alike. They were a shaggy-haired crew, wearing high clogs, with identical plaid blankets over one shoulder, their identifying mark: *sōshi*, thugs hired by a local politician, out to avenge the crippling of the boss' crony. They howled for the fat man and the master of the establishment, who had already left for the magistrate's office to pay the bribe. Finding neither, they battered their way from room to room. Given that the men in the rooms were the ones who kept their boss in power, they merely went through the motions—their clubs, goads, sending them running half naked out into the street. They took out their borrowed rage on the whores, for in truth, they didn't give a damn about the old samurai in the ditch.

Eventually, three men crashed into one room and found the two blind women, standing quietly against one wall. Unlike the whores, they had dressed for the road at the first sounds of trouble, and though indoors, had also tied straw sandals on their feet. The younger of the two was quiet, head down, simply standing and breathing. The elder was mumbling to herself, and one of the men swaggered up, "You old bitch! What did you say? Speak up! We want to fuck your daughter here, or whoever she is, and you can watch. Ta-chan, that's a good one, isn't it? The blind old grandma can watch!" He peered under her woven straw hat, gazing into her milky white eyes, and she smiled, a surprising grin of strong white teeth, then raised a clenched hand up towards her mouth. Pursing her lips with a simpering coquettishness that caused his jaw to drop in alarm, she opened her palm and suddenly blew a handful of powder into his eyes. He screamed, staggering backwards and dropped to the floor clutching his face, the sound blending in with those of the raped and beaten whores. One of his friends lunged forwards, swinging his club. The old woman stumbled under the arc of the weapon, and clasped her arms around him. The man deliberately fell on top of her with bone-crushing force, and crossing the lapels of her kimono, began to strangle her. Her right hand brushed her own hair and then reached up feebly to the side of his head, as she convulsed into apparent unconscious. He stiffened, and she brought her hand back to her head, heaving her hips and shrugging his dead body aside. Only the fastest of eyes would have seen her withdraw a long hairpin that she then thrust six inches deep within his ear. Her spasm was a rapid twirl of the needle, which she then withdrew and inserted back into the knot of grey. She rose to her hands and knees, head cocked to one side, listening, feeling precisely one tatami to the side for her staff, and as the third and final man attacked, she thrust outwards with perfect timing, crushing his throat. As he choked to death on his own blood, she crawled around the floor, brushing any object she encountered with her fingertips. Finding one of the men's clubs, she smashed the skulls of the other two men, one already dead, one still screaming with his fingers desperately wiping his eyes. Then she broke one man's left forearm and another's shoulder. She tugged at the bodies, placing clubs in each of their hands. For all intents and purposes, it would look like the three of them had a falling out and beat each other to death, the man with the crushed larynx apparently surviving last.

She grabbed the passive arm of the Moongirl, snarling that it was time to leave. They walked through the upper hallway, encountering no one until just before the stairs, where one thug, in mid-rape, looked over his shoulder and seeing the two anma pass, shook his head, thinking them either a drunken hallucination, or if real, irrelevant to his current task.

# 22

The Moongirl's days and nights followed a simple round. They would enter a town, and go from inn to inn until they found work. The pleasure quarter never sleeps, and swaying lanterns made the nights almost as bright as the days. They would earn their keep: a few coins, a corner to sleep, and some food to eat. The old woman would use her herbs to treat the sick, and both she and the Moongirl would readjust joints, and work the cramped muscles of whomever had money to pay. Occasionally, the patron's thoughts would turn to sex, but this was not to be. The old woman would smell the lust rising within his flesh, and she would move in as if to help her apprentice, and subtly work his body so that his desire would gutter and flicker out like a candle under glass.

Some men never even knew what had happened and simply drifted off to sleep. Others, who believed that there was no such thing as a massage without a fuck at the end, would stomp off, throwing down a few coins, only a portion of the money he owed, pursued by the snarls of the old woman.

They also spent time in the woods, and the Moongirl began to learn herbs by touch, by smell and in very small amounts, because so many were poisonous, by taste. She learned to map her steps, to remember the twists her body made as she rounded a tree, to compensate for a downhill or uphill slope, to remember sounds and smells from far away. She had no idea where she was, but she was, in one sense, no longer lost. She could find her way back to where she had been, and, in addition to the medicinal, could recognize edible leaves and roots by touch and smell.

The nights were for sleeping, if they were not in a lighted town. Brigands lurked the roads in the dark, and two women alone would be assumed to be easy prey. She was then tied to the old

woman, arm-to-arm, who would awaken at the slightest movement, alert for any attempt to escape, a desire that, along with
her will, her voice, and her previous life, the Moongirl seemed
to have lost.

There was one other activity to which much time was devot-
ed. Whenever they were alone, the old woman would strip her
naked, and perform anma upon her. Not for sex. Never that.
She simply taught the young woman everything she knew:
how to set a dislocated shoulder and how to dislocate it in the
first place; how to render a man unconscious or impotent, if
he decide to put his mark on her after the massage; pressure
that healed, and points that caused pain; the strokes that
untangled cramped muscles, and shakes and adjustments that
reset the nervous system of the injured. "See, this point here,
it clears the lungs, but don't press too hard, it'll lose its effect.
Just here, yes, doesn't that hurt? I'll give you credit, most men
would be screaming. I could kill you now, I'd have to shove
just right, see? That's just a little, it feels like your rib is going
to stab through your liver, doesn't it? Stop moaning. I can
take it away by twisting here and here, and a tug of the leg.
Isn't the human body the most remarkable thing? You don't
breathe right. Did you know that? Yes, because your shoulder
got twisted, and you've got that scar tissue over the rib cage,
I can fix that—like this and this and this. As strong as your
hands are getting, you can take his life if you can get a hold of
him. Soon it'll be the same with your walking staff. You can
smell the weak areas of a man and feel them too. You smell
his breath, and you thrust two thumbs underneath; there's
his throat. Or right into the stink of his crotch, and burst his
bladder. His heartbeat you can hear, and a hand's breadth
lower and a little bit to his left is the notch of his ribs, and a
thrust with your fingertips, deep enough there will freeze him
in his tracks. See? Can't breathe, can you. Don't worry, your
breath will come back, unless I thrust so deeply that I manage
to tear the blood vessel right here."

The old woman knew that those who are owned sometimes want to escape or even kill their captor, but she believed there to be no danger. She was at home in her blindness, like a fish in the sea, while the Moongirl had to hide, her life in perpetual shadow.

Even the waning moon, however, is never extinguished. Completely in the earth's shadow, it rises, a black pearl in a blacker sky. When the old woman found her, she was nearly starved to death, mad with grief and terror. Her mind was still untethered, yawing and slipping, from a chaotic whirl of knife slashes in pitch dark to nursing her baby while rocking in her bear-man's arms. Her brutal rebirth at the hands of the old woman was more of the same: the shock of icy water—that unimaginable pain followed by her blissful wrapping in the womb of her flesh—all intertwined with more jagged bolts of hatred, fear and chaos within. Her sun-blindness was more knife-slashes, light more agonizing than the Mantis' obsidian blade.

Yet strangely, the old woman began to give her back to herself. Her hands on the Moongirl's body was a new language, as was the taste of the autumn air, the touch of the hairy vine that cured headache, and the sound of geese flying overhead to Siberia. More than anything else, the death of that village cur was, strangely, a moment of peace. Her terror that this was her wolf-dog followed at her relief that he was not, cut through the pandemonium of memories and pain. Amidst the fear for her child, her grief for her man, and her self-hatred at her inability to do anything to save either of them, she remembered herself. She remembered a word spoken both in love and then in sadistic glee: "Live."

Yet she was helpless, wasn't she? Blinded by light, even the candle in a red-paper lantern was too much for her. Invisibly, however, she began to acquire a new being, because every fact, be it the sensation of a thumb smoothing the web of fascia under her collarbone, or a touch with her walking staff delicate enough to reveal blades of grass on the ground, mapped out the world she now lived. Bit by bit, like seams of quartz within volcanic rock, this awareness threaded itself, a scaffolding of sound, touch and smell within the whirlwind visions of her tortured mind.

And one more thing.

Sight.

At night, lying beside the road, tied to the old woman who snored and snarled her way through her dreams, she would part the wings of raven that covered her eyes. In the night, her sensitized eyes drank in the slightest variations of light and dark; for her, the needles of pine-trees were edged in star-frost, and footprints in the moss on the forest floor were pools darker than black. Once, crossing a brook, she gazed down into what should have been a ribbon of ink, and she saw fish, not merely shadows, but eyes, scales and filigreed fins.

She lay in the grass, bundled in her kimono, her eyes flinching even from the light of the constellations, turning to drink in the pouring torrent of shadows, a refuge from the explosions of agony that reigned colorful in her memories. In this new world of black and silver and shade, through thoughts still fragmented and broken, a second word arose within her, one which she whispered silently into the night: "Wait. Wait. Wait. Live. Wait. Wait."

# 23

Had the two women merely been walking together or sitting quietly near the road, perhaps things would have been different. Perhaps the dog in him would have yelped, and he would have leapt upon her, whimpering and squirming and licking her face. And then he would have died, for the old woman would have smelled him, heard him and killed him, breaking his spine while he swarmed into the Moongirl's arms, all uncaring if she broke one of her arms or ribs in the process—those could be fixed. And the pain? Life is pain.

But it was not that way. He had searched for seasons, and lost her scent time and time again as she dissolved into the smells of a town, or vanished altogether while crossing a stream. It took him months to heal, and he starved in areas where most of the game was too fast or too strong for his weakened body. The wolf in him won, however, and eventually, he was himself, deep chested and lithe, the loss of the use of one leg of little consequence. He could not catch an animal at full run, but he was quiet and canny, finding the deer where they lay in sleep; hearing the mice when they ran under the snow and pouncing upwards, hovering, then descending, jaws first, to grab a mouthful of fur and meat and bone, sneezing out the snow and clamping down. He stole from foxes and badgers, and if they did not perceive him approaching, killed and ate them as well.

He had followed her to the outskirts of a small town, shying away from the noise of the people, skulking around in the fields outside, waiting for her to emerge. In the middle of the night, a north wind wafted her scent to him. His hair rose on his neck and he bared his fangs, for what he smelled was fear and rage. Soon after, she came slowly down the road with the other, who smelled of alpha fury. "This has gone on long enough! I hate them all, but at least I can be silent. You cannot. There we were, a rich man under your hands, all happy, with nothing on his mind but an easing of his aching back, and what do you do? What do you do! You start mumbling about your man, your man and your boy, and who wants a madwoman putting her hands on them? No one! That's who! We have no coin, we have nothing!" Around a bend and out of sight of the village, she backhanded the Moongirl across the face, and when she fell, raised her staff high above her head to smash her across the hips.

He made no sound, but with the wind behind them, she smelled him at the last second, and tried to turn. It was too late. Just as he would take a deer, he bit one ankle, cutting deeply into the tendon. No longer a puppy, he had learned from the Mantis, and he used his teeth like a blade rather than a vice, slashing and moving out of range. As she twisted to strike him, her tendon snapped, the sound a small explosion in the night. Unstrung, she fell on top of the Moongirl. The wolf-dog circled around snarling, trying to find an angle of attack, but this was impossible, because the two women erupted.

The Moongirl, too, had smelled the beast. Go home, my reader, and upon entering the house where you were born, the smell will carry you back to a day where you fell and ran crying to huddle in your mother's arms. Smell your lover's skin and remember that night when he first rocked you. Stand in a pine forest, and let that creosote sting sweep you to the artist's studio, the turpentine wreathing your hair as you picked out that picture that hangs over your bed.

Her blindness gave her gifts. She could smell moods and seasons—and she could certainly smell her own beast.

As the old woman fell, the Moongirl twisted like an adder, jackknifing to her side, then twisted again, her hands, already bear-killing strong, now exquisitely precise, finding the map of the old woman's nerves, who writhed and screamed at the Moongirl's touch. She threw herself aside, and reaching into her kimono, pulled out a blade. "So you've been waiting all this time.

You ungrateful bitch. I own your life. Give it back to me."

The Moongirl tore the wings of hair from her eyes, whipping backwards to avoid the silver fang of the old woman's dagger. There she was, crouching, a twisted tree-root, her kimono rucked about her stout thighs with black blood pouring from her ankle. And there was her wolf-dog, glowing silver, crouching low, teeth bared and snarling, about to pounce, very likely onto the point of her blade. "Sssst," the sound she used to make to keep her dogs from rushing into the jaws of a cornered bear. He growled, holding still. The Moongirl stood up and walked forward, watching in the dark, deliberately going close, observing how the old woman, lamed, could only crab-crawl towards her, tracking her every move, but unable to stand.

She stepped backwards and spoke. "No. I am all mine" touching herself over the heart, "not yours. Mine. Listen while I walk away."

She and the wolf-dog began to walk towards the mountains, skirting widely around the old woman, dangerous still. The Moongirl moved mercury-smooth, stepping in pools of shade and shadow, and silvery glowing starlight. She kept her own staff, for night would only gift her sight so long. The wolf-dog pressed his body tight against her leg. They could hear the woman screaming after her, dragging herself back towards the town, her voice as bereft as a newborn left on a rubbish heap. Only when the night was silent did she crouch down and the wolf-dog swarmed over her, wriggling and squirming, licking her, whimpering, grabbing limbs in his terrible jaws, then letting go and squirming some more, she silent, with tears running down her cheeks.

# River

A boy and a lean thing shaped like a man dive into a cascade, a rapid that roars through a ravine, lit by narrow beams of sunlight that pierce their way through the trees and rocks. The waves are sometimes as high as a horse's head, smashing into boulders and downed trees. The man-thing slithers past, as graceful as an otter. The boy is drowning. He is smashed over and over into the rocks. Finally the man-thing reaches out and holding his face above the waves, embraces him closely as they go through together. The rapids end in a waterfall, and they spill outward into the air to land in a quiet pool below. The boy is unconscious. The Mantis carries him out, and slinging him over his shoulder, climbs back to the top of the rapids. He slaps him awake, throws him in, then follows. They have been at this for sixteen days. Each day the boy gets a little further before he begins to drown.

# 24

Kenko drifted northwards into snow country. He'd gotten another job after the incident with the old samurai. This one went even more badly than the last, once he got in a fight with a *yakuza* gang. One of their underbosses raped a girl who was more than willing to fuck for coin, but the bastard only got hot when he saw blood. Kenko dropped by to pay a visit. Because the police would be all over anyone who fought with swords, the gang kept them locked away, only to be used in times of 'war.' They used to hang around a small stable—the boss had a horse he loved far more than his children—so they claimed to be farriers, even did a little horseshoeing on the side to keep up appearances. They kept a brazier filled with red-hot coals with a number of iron pokers thrust deep into the glowing fire, just in case anyone dropped by. That was probably the best fight ever! He'd only brought a tree-limb, and there were four of them. Got a nasty burn on the back of a thigh. If he hadn't moved, he'd have been spit-roasted from the inside out. Four pokers deserved four broken shoulders, with two skulls and one hip for good measure. And the underboss: crushed his kneecaps to gravel, and his testicles to mush. Turned out the head boss was into politics too, this one a Diet member. It seemed to be in vogue—claim to love your country, and all your sins were forgiven. Osaka in the south to well north of Tokyo was now out of bounds to him. There was no official warrant for his arrest, because the yakuza wanted an extra-judicial solution, but the police were more than happy to keep an eye out on their behalf. The reward for him to be brought back to the stable, trussed up like a boar all ready for the grill, was high enough that half the gamblers and all of the police in the Kanto plain would give up their eyeteeth for a chance to catch him.

He got hired again in a brothel near the copper mines. This was as low as he'd sunk in a long time. The miners were a hard lot, stinking of sweat and earth before they started drinking, and then, barely able to stand, they'd get it in their head that they deserved a woman. The women were their match. He had to thump a couple of heads every night, men and women both. He'd finally close the doors right before dawn, get a bottle of sake and unwind with one of the women, all of whom by now were reeking of sweat, earth and semen.

Kenko always paid his way. They could simply refuse his coin if they didn't want him. If they didn't have a good time, at least his good time wasn't nasty, just a quick ride. He'd hear plenty of hard-luck stories; most of these women had been sold by their own parents to ward off starvation, as well as giving them one less mouth to feed. Others had run from abusive men, or had a husband die on them, soon followed by getting kicked off their land.

This night he was royally drunk. Sometimes, the best way to avoid a fight, particularly with a big boy who might damage the premises, was to pour him a cup of sake or two or three, and match him drink for drink. It'd been one of those nights.

There was a new girl, probably in her mid-twenties, and although his vision was blurry, she was a tall strong woman with thick eyebrows and pale white skin. He tromped up to her room. She was just washing herself, her kimono askew, scrubbing her pussy with an expression of tired disgust. He stood at the doorway, watching, and slurred out, "You have energy for one more? I'm the owner's strong-arm." She looked at him, irritated.

"No, no, you don't have to. I pay my way. I wouldn't thump heads for free either—well, that's not true—but I know you are a working girl, so I'm buying, not taking, if you want my coin."

Folding his hand back into his kimono sleeve, he pulled out a fistful, three times the asking price. Her expression of irritation deepened, but he knew his women. "I know it's more than the usual, but all I'm asking for is the usual."

She laughed. "Alright, big man. You want to spend your money on a tired whore, that's your choice. The girls say you are as big down . . ." her eyes widened as he parted his kimono with a grin, and staggered into the room like a rotund tripod, teetering on only two of its legs.

She knelt on her futon and stroked him hard, then said, "You lie there. I'll be safer with that monster if I'm the one doing the riding." He happily rolled back, and as she sat astride him, his mind wandered to those nights in the fields, farmer's wives astride him in clouds of fireflies. Swept away in memory and sake, his head filled with the smell of her. She was a talker, too, this one—"Oh, gods, you are a stallion, you big man, yes, you just lie there and make it throb, I'm not going to move, oh no, you have to work, but don't you move either. You think you have skills, you mighty cocksman, you? How about this, I can clench as much as you can swell. Us Kozuke girls don't lose to anyone!"

Through the fog of his half-unconscious ecstasy, he heard the last phrase and heard her accent too. She sounded like home.

"Girl, where are you from?"

"Kumagaya, danna? You ever heard of it?"

He grew still. She was just the right age. And that face! They both had that plump face, the same as his. She was a big girl, just like his daughters. They were always a head taller than the other girls! It could be either—Rei or Sachi— they were born just one year apart. He closed his eyes, hoping he'd wake up on his own pallet, alone.

"Danna, you OK? You fall asleep? Hey, look, if you want to sleep, go to your own bedding. I've got to get some rest, those miners won't be back 'til nightfall, but some of the merchants like to come in for a mid-day ride. Wake up, danna. Wake up!"

He groaned. "Kumagaya, you say?" Then, slowly, whispering,

he asked, "Your name isn't Oshima, is it?"

"What? Oshima? No. There were lots of Oshima's around—I remember that. No, I'm a Matsumoto. We were farmers. A lot of my family used to live around Sakai. Anyway, we got kicked off our land after Meiji. My mother had six of us, and then my pa died, and she sold three of us off, so she could make a new start with the little ones. There are a lot of Oshima in Kumagaya, aren't there? Why, are you from around there?"

He shook his head as fast as he could. "No, no. . . . no. I just knew a guy, once, from there. It's the only name I know."

"OK, well do you want to fuck or reminisce? I'm too tired to talk and as for fucking, if you wouldn't mind finishing? I sort of lost track of where we were going, and I don't think I'm going to get it back. It doesn't happen all that much, anymore. You start doing something for work, and it stops being much fun."

He picked her hips up, and his prick, soft, slid out of her like a very tired and disconsolate python. "No, I think I'm just too drunk tonight. Another time."

He washed himself with the same cloth she'd used, and blearily trudged out of the room, the earthenware bottle of sake dangling from one enormous finger. He was shaken. "It could have been one of mine. There's nothing wrong with being a whore. Hell, I like whores. But, thank the gods she wasn't my daughter—I don't even want to think about that." He began pounding his head. "I'm drunk, I'm drunk, and I'm tired. It was just the voice from home that got me. But think! What if Rei or Sachi was a whore? Not that I'd be fucking them!" He punched that thought out of his head. "I mean, I like whores, I like women, I like fucking, other men like fucking, women like fucking—OK, not usually when they are whores—but they like the money and they don't have any other way, and they aren't bad for being whores, and they usually end up whores when something bad has happened to them, like their man beats them one too many times, or their family dies, or their father runs out and leaves the family

86

without any way to make . . . ."

"Well, is it wrong if my daughters are whores? Why is it wrong?
We all fuck: some do it for free, some take money and some give
money, and what's better than fucking anyway? The world's an
ugly place, and for just a moment, you find yourself in a cloud of
fireflies under the stars with a woman sliding up and down, the
scent of her and the scent of wild-flowers, and can't that happen
for whores too? Not that they spend much time out under the
stars, they are usually under some stinking copper miner, or
sooner or later, some woman-beating, ass-fucking monster. *Chi-
kusho*! Who has fucked my Rei-chan? Who has fucked my Sachi?
I used to stick out my arms and they'd laugh like little sparrows
and hang, one on each index finger, I was the only man who
could swing them that way. Their mouths were like little flower
buds, and they'd giggle, and every time I came home, they'd
be so happy that their daddy was home. They used to climb in
my arms, and we'd go walking down the street and they were
so proud because no one could scare them, because they were
with their papa." He slumped against the doorframe, and began
to weep, a bawling, drunken fat man. The sake bottle slipped
from his finger and broke on the ground. He punched himself a
tremendous blow to the forehead. It didn't knock him out, but it
hurt like hell, so he did it again and a third time. The pain drove
nothing away. He slid down to the floor and fell asleep.

# 25

"Hey, Kenko. Wake up. What the hell is wrong with you? You can't sleep here, right in view of the town! We have to clean up, and here you are, sprawled out in the entranceway with your prick hanging out. By the gods, that thing belongs in a shrine to be carted out for the festival, not attached to a man! *Kuso!* You and your prick—I swear, that's where your brains are, a dick pulling a man around after it! You gotta clean up! You're supposed to keep drunks out of this place, and you're the drunk you have to keep out. And who the hell punched you? You've got a black eye and a bruise across half your head. What's the reputation of this place going to be if my *yojimbo* gets his ass kicked? The miners are going to tear this place up. What the fuck is wrong with you?"

Kenko blearily opened his eyes. He saw three of the little man. He considered reaching up and taking the man's throat between his finger and thumb, and pinching until the voice turned into a squeak, but he couldn't figure out which one to pinch first. And two of them would still be talking. He closed his eyes again, and the man bent over him, shaking his shoulder. Ahh. There he was. Kenko reached up and covered the man's nose and mouth, put the other hand behind his head and squeezed so tightly that he imagined the top of his skull would pop off, and his brains would come fizzing out like a poorly fermented batch of sake. After a while, the man's struggles began to slow down, and Kenko released him. He dropped to his hands and knees, sucking air. Kenko leaned forward, and put his hand gently under the man's chin. "I can't do this anymore."

The man coughed and gasped. Kenko gently patted him on the back with the other hand. The man choked out, "You mean drink? That's probably a good idea."

"No, danna. I mean this. All of this. I can't do—this" (waving an arm around him, taking in the brothel, the tavern, the town, all of it) "anymore."

He heaved himself to his feet, then helped up the owner and brushed off his clothes. Rolling his shoulders like a mournful bull, he stomped back to his living quarters, gathered his things and walked down the road.

# 26

The Moongirl lived in the night. As long as she did not look directly at her sister in the sky, she was at ease. Whatever her intentions, the old woman had healed her. Her terrible hands had broken up the webs of scar tissue underneath her old wounds, and since escaping and once again hunting prey, she had become as powerful and graceful as her man used to be. Still dayblind, she would find a place to sleep before dawn, hiding from both sun and mankind. Her wolf-dog would come and go as he pleased, often hunting during the day, but he never went far. As the sun went down, the cool fingers of dusk would caress her cheek and she would awaken to a world of stars and shade. She became the best hunter of her age, because she could now see the wild boar asleep in a thicket, or a monkey in the crotch of a tree. Animals hide through dappling of colors and patterns that break up their form, but with night eyes, all that was irrelevant, not even perceived. Instead, she saw dark within dark, a shadow among the leaves, and sometimes, the tip of each hair reflecting starlight. The moon rose in the eyes of the deer, and footprints pressed down in the forest loam were pools of black amidst charcoal. She sometimes had to travel during the daylight, so she bound her hair over her eyes and wore a wicker hat that covered most of her face over that, just another blind masseuse as far as others were concerned. Her nose and her ears remained keen— she could tell the difference between the footsteps of a child from that of a man or woman at a hundred yards, and knew from the smells of food, sweat, incense and pomade that surrounded them, if they were farmer, merchant or samurai class.

Her memories were inescapable; her previous joys all the more painful, because whatever she recalled, it all ended in the same terrible apocalypse. Her mind would explode in a maelstrom: her lonely childhood, her escape, her love, his love, his death, her joy, her child, her child, her child, her helplessness. Still helpless. Despite her skills as a huntress, she knew as sure as the sun's daggers in her eyes that were she to encounter the Mantis now and try to rescue her son, she would fail and he would suffer all the more. But she was not defeated. "Live," she would whisper, "Live. Wait. Wait. Live."

# 27

Early fall, and the trees on the mountain slopes were just turning color. Kenko wandered the forest paths, walking towards the coast. He needed to smell the sea or a powerful river—needed the thunder of something powerful drowning out what wouldn't leave his head.

The maples were aflame, and the birch trees, yellow, with trunks as white as bone. There were lots of fir trees as well, sometimes whole forests, green and astringent, with that turpentine smell of sap, and in other places, just bamboo. At this time of the year, a lot of the latter were dried out, and as the cold autumn wind rushed through them, they'd rustle and hiss. Sometimes, he'd just start barreling around, setting them clashing and clonking against one another, the tops swaying above.

There were lots of mushrooms on the forest floor, amanitas in particular, red or brown caps with white warts. If you wanted dreams that might take you so far into the next world that you might never come back, that was the way to go, but he had waking nightmares enough already. Sober many months, his thoughts still looped around; men like him created women like those he paid to fuck. He was the father who betrayed the daughters who got sold to men who turned them into whores to whom he was kind, all the while condemning the men who didn't fuck them nicely like he did. His stomach clenched at what felt like the most narrow of escapes—what if she had been his daughter? But was it any better that she wasn't? She was someone's daughter and, what kind of man would be happy with his daughter dancing on the end of my prick for a few coins."

His head hurt all the time, and he never felt so tired. He could hear his breath wheezing in his chest and his feet shuffling through the leaves. A nightingale, curious about the fat man, followed him, hidden in the bushes, singing its sweet and piercing song. As always, he couldn't see it—a drab little bird singing its melody, a cascade of notes out of nowhere.

Nightfall. Tree frogs started to sing too, little lime-green fellows with red eyes, calling out to any girl frog for a ride, chirping, "How big, how big, how big I am, how big, how big, how big I am, how big, how big, how big I am." Kenko smiled a little, seeing the irony, little guys no bigger than his thumbnail, with exactly the same attitude as his. The moment passed, and he again sank into his misery.

He kept walking north and eventually, he arrived at the coast. The sea was grey and harsh and the wind, just starting its eight month sweep from the Siberian plains, freezing cold and full of sleet. This was as good a place as any.

Time passed: weeks, months, a couple of years. He worked as a laborer on the docks, his strength unchanged. He was not celibate, but he no longer fucked whores. He was sure that he must have made children—more girls destined to become whores, he thought, and more pricks to fuck them—and he didn't want to do that anymore, so occasionally, if he got the nod, he would sneak into the homes of older women, widows, long past child-bearing age. Even then, he thought of his daughters—and increasingly of his wife, once a laughing girl, then a put-upon dried up bitch. "And whose fault was that?" he'd think. "The first time we fucked, she looked at me and said, 'I could do this forever with you.' We were married, and that first six months, that was a sweet time, wasn't it? Then I came home one morning, singing, drunk, the smell of a woman all over me, and something broke inside her. I saw it. It broke as clean and clear as an icicle snapping off the eaves and shattering on the ground. I kept right on going, doing what I was doing. She was a good girl: tried to accept things the way they were. We kept fucking, had the girls, and each time—snap—snap—snap—snap—until there was nothing more to break. And all it did was piss me off. I didn't want to come home and listen to her bitch about this and that, and there

94

were so many sweet women who didn't want to bitch at all, just sneak out and have a little something to take themselves away from what they were bitching about at home." So these days he fucked the widows, no harm could come of that, he thought, but they always wanted more, and they'd get mournful or angry or cold, and what a sorry mess. Nothing had any flavor anymore.

He thought he'd feel better, now that he was doing the right thing. He continued to feel worse. He couldn't conceive of returning home. Even if they wouldn't arrest him—or kill him—he could only imagine the sight of him would destroy whatever peace his family had bought. His wife was probably long remarried—her new husband would not be happy to see him, and if he were an asshole, she'd get a beating for it. His daughters had probably accepted the mystery. What did he have to show for all his years of wandering anyway? Worst of all, what if he returned and found that they had been sold as whores? No, that wasn't the worst. What if he returned home and learned that they disappeared, that they were just . . . . . . . . . . . .gone? That they did to him what he did to them, simply left a hole in the air, an absence laden with unanswerable questions and regrets.

He was working as a night watchman, guarding a storehouse from the peasants who grew the rice that the merchant bought. Now that they were starving, they wanted it back, but they were too hungry to riot. So all he did was sit near a fire and occasionally make his rounds.

"I can break just about any man over my knee, and I can fuck any woman and roll her eyes right back into her head. Men like me, we can take whatever we want, and we are powerful beyond most other men, so if we decide something's right—or right for us—we just do it. I feel like I walked out on a frozen pond, and all I wanted to do was slip and slide around the surface, and suddenly it broke and in I went. I'm under the ice now, aren't I? People can look through and see my hands and face pressing up against the milky surface of the ice, but it's too thick to break though. It's cold. It's so cold, and I'm on the other side, all alone."

For the first time in ages, he remembered the jujutsu dojo in the village of Kumagaya, all the gnarled old men, and tough young men who tried to take them down. He remembered the pain, to be sure, because such men play rough, but mostly, he remembered the laughter. He'd just met Kishi, he was sixteen years old and she a year younger, and he had honest labor, honest practice, and the fucking was honest too. Those were the best times he ever had. A hard day's work, and all you wanted was a soak in the bath and some sleep, but you'd drag yourself to the dojo and as soon as you clapped your hands and bowed to the small shrine at the front, all the tiredness would drop away. They'd do sumo to get the blood flowing and get an attitude adjustment as well. Sumo was the most honest thing in the world—you couldn't bullshit winning and losing—and getting dropped in the dirt or doing the same to someone else, that was all it took. And then home to Kishi, and for a brief time, truth there too. But after he came into his strength, he cut himself off from the other men, even fucked a few of their wives, just because he could, even though they were good men and thought they were his friends.

What was true now? He couldn't stand being in the town. He hated to see men with their noses open, drunk and bawling for pussy. People—their lusts, their desires, and the stupid things they said simply reminded him of himself, and he'd do anything not to be himself any more.

He took to wandering in the forests. Eventually, up a side valley not too far from the Hottai waterfall, he built a small hut: comfortable, overlooking a small clear stream that laughed its way down the valley. It was similar to earth dwellings of the *tsuchigumo*, legendary people who lived in Japan two thousand years before. The floor was about three feet below the earth's surface, which allowed it to hold the warmth of the hearth, and it was covered with a vaulted thatch roof. He pounded the floor almost as hard as rock, and covered this with slabs of slate. The land was unclaimed, and in small clearings, he planted dry-land millet, and daikon and other greens; the forests were full of mushrooms and game, and after awhile, he ceased to go into town, and let hunger, cold and self-loathing scour the flesh from his bones.

Best of all was the waterfall, underneath which he would stand. The weight was huge, and the differential pressure of the water forced him to make constant micro-adjustments in his stance. It was like fighting with the heart of the mountain, a being that never tired, that beat him to his knees no matter how often he stood up again. Finally, he'd collapse and it would spit him out in the pool below, no more than he deserved.

# Fruit

The oak trees are red, and the persimmon trees are laden with balls of orange. One tree bears a strange fruit. There is a boy with one arm tied to his side, the other gripping a branch. He hangs unmoving, silent. Occasionally a horsefly alights on his naked body. Her mouthparts are like scissors, and the blades slash open a small wound, pooling with blood, which the fly laps up with her tongue to feed her babies. Tomorrow, he will hang by the other arm.

# 28

She began walking towards home. Entering a small village in the darkest portion of the night, she stole food and a tattered old kimono. In the house of the headman, a merchant, she found two gold *ryō*, oblong coins, and slipped them into the folds of her clothes. She wandered from hut to hut, listening to people sleeping and left, feeling more ghost than human. She bit her own wrist to prove to herself that she was alive, but this proved nothing. Maybe the world of the dead was teeth in the flesh, so she hugged the wolf-dog, inhaling his scent and digging her fingers into his thick fur. She knew that no god of hell would give her the comfort of such an animal, and she returned to herself and some tenuous peace.

Reaching the mountains, she and her wolf-dog began to climb. It was autumn once again, and the lower slopes were aflame with color, but its beauty was now lost to her. They glided through the trees, past charcoal burners asleep on pallets of straw, hunting boar and deer, gathering roots and vegetables to round out her meals.

She made a bone needle, and she took out the stitches of the stolen kimono and sewed the fabric into the quilted pantaloons and jacket of the matagi. She demolished her straw hat, and rewove it into something better suited to shed the snow. She trapped *tanuki*, raccoon dogs, one after another, and tanned their hides with their own brains, a several week process that kept her bound to one spot, a small cave in the rocks, just below the tree line. She frayed their leg tendons and made them into fine cord, which she used to sew mittens, fur pantaloons and a cape. She killed a deer with a fire-hardened spear, which she made by touch, burning the end of the wood, letting it cool, feeling its shape, then burning it some more, all with her eyes closed, not even turning her head towards the flames. From the deer, she took more tendons that she separated, then braided into a bow-string, and hooves that she boiled for glue. From this, she made a short laminated bow from deer horn and bamboo.

One night her wolf-dog ran off and later, she saw him dancing, mating in a clearing with another dog, a *matagi inu* like his moth-er. She left them to their joy, and walking in concentric circles, quiet as a snake on moss, she found the dog's master asleep under a small lean-to. He was old, yet smelled much like her own man, and silently weeping, she stole his blade, the socketed spear-knife, then feebly reached out a hand towards his sleeping face in apology. She placed the two gold coins at the tip of his spear shaft, a near fortune to a man such as he. Then she walked on, knowing her wolf-dog would find her when he finished his adventure.

They entered the Alps right before a snowstorm and they had a hellish descent down a mountainside, a whiteout blizzard that lowered visibility to nothing. She found another cave, and lay there huddled with the wolf-dog, warm, but shaking with agony at the returning visions of murderous loss.

Nightfall, three days later, she broke through the snow block-ing the entrance, and she and the wolf-dog began crossing the mountains. Ferocious winds roared from the continent, flying over the sea, only to be grabbed by the claws of the mountains, leaving snow well over head-height, and prone to avalanche. Descending one mountain did not liberate her from this world of granite and ice. It only offered her another mountain to climb. Often she had to carry her wolf-dog, because the ascent, at times, was up ledges and handholds of bare rock. She would hoist the animal so his side rested on her back-pack, a frame of wood with a bundle of everything she owned, and then would lightly tie his three paws together and loop them around her neck, the fourth curled tightly upwards against his chest, leaving her hands free. The wolf-dog was uncharacteristically still, accepting this with equanimity, gazing about him with curiosity, even as his weight threatened to topple her backwards as she clung with fingertips and toes to the face of a cliff. Over and over again, the blizzards blew in, and over and over again, they had to huddle under shelter to survive. Sometimes, approaching a snowfield, he whimpered and refused to go on, and when she went ahead, he uncharacteristically barked, for he was a silent animal. Trusting him, she would slowly back up the slope to where he waited. On one occasion, the snow slipped away and poured down the mountain, a droning rumbling hum echoing back up the valley, two hundred feet tall cedars and crytomeria in jackstraw jumble amidst the snow.

It was not a straight line over the backbone of the land. Several times, they came to cliffs that offered only a leap into the void, or traveled up valleys that ended in impenetrable walls of drifted snow. At times, even with a clear path, there was clearly no game, and starving, they would have to retreat to lower ground to kill a deer or *kamoshika*, a goat-antelope, to gorge on fresh meat and dry the rest.

They took a fork to the northwest, and as late spring finally broke through winter's grip, they wandered up a peninsula of land, it too, spined by mountains which descended on each side to rocky cliffs and down to the sea. The waves boomed and rushed back, and rocks rattled and clashed.

# Mouse

*He waits besides a clearing in the forest. It is midnight. A mouse wanders out into the open space, and an owl, absolutely silent, sweeps down and grabs her within his talons. An instant later, the boy leaps upward, grabbing the two legs of the bird, and wrenches the mouse from its grasp. He lands, rolls and flings the bird upwards, its beak missing his face. He shoves the mouse into his mouth and crunches down on it, sucking it dry of its blood, while dodging the enraged owl's repeated attacks.*

# 海女
「Ama」

# 29

Why the sea? For most of us, the setting sun is a little death: an entrance to the dark world of sleep, the unseen, the unknown. For the Moongirl, the dying of light was a rebirth. The sun's rising at her back drove her onwards, and with its descent each evening, the cool night caressed her skin and drew her into its loving arms. North was her child and west was freedom, and thus, somehow, she and her wolf-dog found themselves at a point of land, rocky cliffs overlooking the waves, with fires of an approaching dawn threatening their backs, They had passed small fishing villages here and there, and one big town lay to the north, so she carefully packed away her matagi garb and once again wore her kimono, knowing if she were caught out in the light, she'd have less to explain. She hid her knife in the folds of her clothes, unstrung her bow and wrapped it and her arrows along one side of her pack.

They descended rocky paths down the cliffs, her wolf-dog moving carefully on his three legs. Ash sky, black rocks and blacker sea, the hissing, rattling rocks, and the cry of gulls. She looked about for shelter from the coming light.

They rounded a spit of land onto a beach festooned with seaweed, and she gathered handfuls that burst with juice in her mouth. The wolf-dog suddenly stopped and looked into the water. She turned at his gaze and saw a pale shape moving, just off shore. A young woman stood up, naked but for a white strip of cloth between her legs, luminous amidst the iron-hued waves, dragging a floating wooden bucket. The sun leapt from behind the cliff, and the girl disappeared in a blaze of light.

# Fire

A boy runs through a mountain village with a burning torch in his hand. He sets each home alight. The doors are tied shut. He squats beside a man, both naked, listening silently to the screams, the flames flickering in their eyes.

# 30

"*Obasan! Obasan!* Wait. Don't go. You're an anma, aren't you? You can't see. The rocks are dangerous here! How did you ever get down the cliffs? Wait, Obasan."

The girl ran across the beach towards the Moongirl, who was slowly feeling with her stick, unable to find her way. It had come up too fast. She was lost, scattershot explosions from the sea and the cliffs surrounding her on all sides. This was worse than the fizzing dazzle of sunlight on snow. It burned through her closed eyelids, and tears streamed down her cheeks.

As the girl approached, the wolf-dog pressed his flank against the Moongirl, but he was not tense nor did he growl. "Obasan. Please, let me help you."

She could have brushed her aside. She'd heard the old woman do it often enough, so offensively that most people turned away without looking back. She could have done it kindly, she could have simply tapped her stick and walked on until the girl gave up. After all, she was naked; how far could she follow? She grabbed the ruff of fur at her wolf-dog's neck, and whispered to him to go on, but uncharacteristically, he stopped. She could feel the muscles in his neck shift as he turned and gazed back at the oncoming girl. The Moongirl brushed her hand over his head, and found his ears up and forehead smooth, a look of friendly curiosity. Lost in a whirlwind of light, she stood, waiting.

# 31

Within a crease in the cliffs, a rivulet of fresh water tumbled down the rocks. The girl had made a small hut: driftwood walls and roof, the latter covered with more driftwood weighted down by stones, with the opening facing the sea. The cliff hid it from above—one could only see it head on, from the beach or the sea. At the girl's urging, the Moongirl entered, and facing the wall, let herself be folded into the shade. Were she not so isolated from humanity, she might have considered bandaging her eyes, providing a story about some injury, but she had lost the ability for such glib circumlocution, and all she could do was bind her hair across her face and sit, one arm around her wolf-dog, tears leaking from her closed eyes.

The girl took a large clamshell, and dipping it in a pool at the base of the tiny waterfall, sluiced fresh water over her body, washing off the salt, laughing

"Obasan, if you could see me, you'd wonder, wouldn't you, gathering the fruit of the sea before dawn. I have only a few heartbeats each morning between the night and the day. I don't belong here. If you stay awhile, I'll tell you all about it. I haven't talked to anyone in ever so long, and I don't know the people here. A girl alone might give men ideas, so I try to keep to myself. Here, let me make a fire, we'll have something to eat. I've two fish here. I bet your dog would like that. I've never seen a dog like that, more like a wolf, but I've never seen a wolf, I can't tell if he's fierce or kind, he seems gentle, he won't bite me, will he? Here, dog, here's some fish, and your mistress and I, we'll have some soup, as soon as the fire burns down to coals. I've got my pot, we can put in seaweed and all these shells, I've got clams, oysters, and abalone, even crow-wing mussels, people don't eat them much, they taste too strong, they say, but I learned to eat them when I was hungry, and now I like them, oh, you'll stay, won't you? Won't you? You'll get hurt if you leave, please stay, I have to get my bucket, I'll be right back." Her words overflowed, like water from a pot of rice set too close to the flames, and as she ran down the beach to grab the wooden bucket, she continued talking, her voice receding and ascending, giving an illusion to the Moongirl that she herself was moving further and further away, then, closer and closer again.

Once again in the hut, she bubbled brightly, yet there was something frantic, something desperate in her, unsettling both woman and dog. Suddenly, as she'd say to her wolf-dog, "Sssttttt!"

"What? What did you say, obasan?"

Voice harsh, creaking from disuse. "Hush, girl. I will stay, but only if you be silent for a while. You are too fast for me."

"I'm sorry, but it's been so long."

"Hush. We will wait, us three. We will wait, we will eat your soup, and we will wait. I have not talked to a girl like you since I was a girl like you. When you are quiet, you can tell me."

"How can I tell you when I'm quiet?"

"Hush now."

Not knowing she would do any such thing, the woman turned slightly, even though the sunlight once again scalded her closed eyes, and opened her left arm, a crescent curve. Long moments. The girl slid across the sandy floor and nestled there, crying.

Wolf and child in the arms of the moon.

# Dragonfly

*Dragonflies flicker over a field, three inches in length, bodies barred yellow and black. A boy wanders among them. The scent of wildflowers. The dragonflies dart and hover, suddenly jetting away, disturbed by currents of air. The boy pauses, leaps and spins, catching a dragonfly gently in each hand. Alighting, he lets them go. Again and again, his body glowing gold and pink in the light of the summer sun.*

# 32

There was no reason to stay, but she couldn't leave. She sat in the dark, and turning her back to the still glowing coals of the fire, listened to the child breathing, silent at last. She smelled of salt, of fish and smoke, and she sighed and stirred in her sleep. The Moongirl let the coals burn down, and then, feeling the air cool, unbound her hair and looked at her face.

The girl was thin, half starved really. She must have lost all her extra flesh in the last winter, the offerings of the sea not enough to fill her out. She was little more than a child, her face still tender. Her lips were pursed, and suddenly the Moongirl remembered her own son, a baby, his mouth pursed in just the same way as he nuzzled for her breast.

The girl began to moan and cry, something terrifying her, and the Moongirl slid close and tenderly ran her fingers along her cheek. Since her resurrection by the old woman, she had touched countless people, but this was the first time since the horror in the snow cave that she did so willingly. The girl moaned louder, and the Moongirl began to sing, her voice creaking, feeling as if she was tearing a scar deep within, and then, finding the line, a gentle melody threaded amidst the sound of the waves. The girl opened her eyes, dark pools, tiny pinpoints of starlight reflected within. Then she drifted into a quiet sleep, the next morning remembering nothing.

Night after night, the Moongirl sang her troubled heart to sleep.

# 33

"There's a big town called Wajima around the other side of the peninsula, obasan. My people live in the *ama*-quarter. . . . What? No, 'ama.' Not 'anma,' like you. We are the women of the sea. For as long as anyone can remember, we have lived a different way. During some of the year, our men fish, and we mend nets, and live just like other fisher folk. But on a given day, we take to our boats, and go either to the seven sister islands, or even further out into the sea, to Hegurajima, where we live for months. Our men scull the boats out into the ocean, and the women wear just the white cat, like the one I had on when I came out of the sea. We bring up seaweed and abalone, and we sell it to the mainland people.

We tie a rope to ourselves and carry a big rock, with a rope around it also, to pull us down. The water is blue and clear and sometimes full of colors, fish of all kinds. We put our catch into a bucket, and when our body screams for air, we tug the rope and the man in the boat pulls us up. We breathe. The air is sweet and salty, it tastes like thin seawater. We have a way of breathing, a whistle, it cleans the lungs; two, three, four breaths, our men pull up the rock, and we clasp it in our arms, and we go down, again and again and again.

It's always been the women who dive, because we stay warmer in the water. The ocean is in our blood; all that's hard on land is washed away in the sea. I knew women who dived the day before giving birth. People who don't know are afraid of so much: sharks, jellyfish, what have you. But most sharks don't care about us, they have their own things to hunt, and we say that if a shark does take you, that's because the sea gods want you for their own.

We enter the sea while still tiny girls, and we can see underwater in a way that other people cannot. I think our tears are seawater. Our men love us more than other men love their women because they need us, not just to give birth, but because it's due to us that we all survive. Other people look down on us, because we dive naked and our skin turns brown, and I guess you don't know, because you've never seen it, but people think white skin is refined and dark skin dirty."

# 34

"It is good being an ama, so good. Women and men are different. When I was little, I would go with my father when he was selling seaweed or abalone shell, and I saw the women of the town. They do not care for each other like we do. On the island, the women get up and make a meal, and then go down to the sea. It's even better when the waves are up, because then they don't go out in boats. Instead, we stay together, taking our buckets, climb down the cliffs and dive together off the rocks. We laugh and laugh, everyone knows everything about each other, and you have to trust each other, because if your heart is troubled, you can die when you dive.

The older women can go down ten, maybe even twelve body lengths. I cannot go half as deep. Your breath is screaming in your chest, and your back hurts, it hurts so bad, but you hold it in longer than you believe you can, and you see your sisters and aunts swimming too, and then you rise, you rise into the sunlight, the sea is blue, and the sky is blue.

I tasted my blood once, I cut myself, and it tastes like the sea. I think we are the sea, at least we women are.

My mother got ill, something broke in her lungs and she couldn't dive anymore, and my father, he took me out, me and my older sisters. We had been playing in the ocean since before we could walk; all the girls played the same. There are black rocks all around the island. The waves are not harsh most of the time. We'd throw stones in the water and dive to get them, deeper and deeper we'd go. One day, my father took us out in his boat, and he told us that he knew we were ready. I was scared, but as soon as I went in the water, it was just . . . my home. The cool water, the sunlight flickering on the surface above my head, blue, then green, colder and colder, and darker, fish flickering around, your lungs screaming, but happy, so happy, and afterwards, we stand, all together, and laugh and pour fresh water on

116

our bodies and the sun dries our skin, and . . .

It was perfect there, but not me. There has always been something wrong in me. My mother told me that I was born in the skirts of a typhoon. There was a solid wall of black clouds overhead, and spikes and forks of lightning marching towards the island like a huge centipede on fire. The thunder was so loud that many people's ears started to bleed. Everyone was crying and praying to the Dragon of the Sea, and somehow the gods spared us. The lightening split a huge rock, right near our house. You can see it today there's a slash of white, like the spear of the gods cleft it in two. My mother said the lightning got inside me.

I used to bite her, and I would scream when my sisters sang. The only way she could nurse me was to lie in the shallow water, and with the waves lapping over us, I would suck. I don't know what is wrong in me. Happiness makes me mad. I feel like someone is pulling a shroud over my face, and I cannot breathe. I could not be near the men, because men are men and they like to be bossy, even with us ama, but when I was with my aunties and the other girls, I hated that too. They would be laughing about Mieko, who snores, or how Sa-chan's husband just won't let her alone at night, he has to have it all the time and everyone knows Sa-chan wasn't really complaining, she was bragging, and I just want to scream so loud that the lightning inside of me will shatter the whole island.

So last year, right before the end of our season on the island, I took my father's boat. I didn't know where I was going. I just couldn't stay. It's a long pull to the mainland, it can take most of a day, and then the wind picked up and blew me back off shore. I must have fought it for two days. I was blown entirely to the other side of the peninsula here. I hid the boat. Unless I have someone else to help me dive, there's no use for it.

I started walking and found this place. There's fresh water, and there are lots of shellfish. You can eat them raw, you know. And I saved my father's fishing net from the boat, and I brought a few things with me: flint and steel for fire, a knife and the bar we use to pry abalone from the rocks. I was happy for a few days. I was finally alone. No one could talk about me; no one could talk to me. I didn't have to hear the same stories, and the same laughter.

But winter was so hard here. There's not much snow on the coast here, but it was so cold and wet. But the fish still come to feed and there's seaweed. You think I'm skinny now—you should have seen me just a few months ago. I'm scared though. I almost died, and it was a warm winter, compared to what it has been in years past.

Last spring, I walked inland a couple of times. But people stared at me, they whispered behind their hands, and once a man followed me, he didn't say anything, I ran and hid in the rocks near the cliffs and he never found me. The farmers, they either have hard faces or dull faces, no welcome, no laughter, and I realized that there was no wonderful world to be found, not for a girl of the waves like me.

I cannot go back. When someone steals, they break the harmony of the village. We survive by such harmony. You are under water, and you pull the rope so that your man will haul you up from the bottom. You must know that it will happen without any hesitation. I broke the circle. It is better they think me dead, because if I go back, it will be worse than death. They will turn their backs. No one will speak. I will be as a ghost. I will wander the streets of the village, and no one will see me. I could wander from house to house and hear my aunties talking, hear my sisters and mother laughing, and they will not see me. I know they wept for me then. They would not weep for me now.

If I try to take my mother in my arms, the men will carry me, their faces like stones, and throw me off one of the high cliffs into the sea.

All I can think of is another theft. If I gather enough abalone shell, maybe I can visit one of the buyers late at night, going behind the island's back. If he is greedy enough to cheat the island, he may give me enough money that I can go somewhere. But I don't know where I would go, what I would do, and maybe he would just take the shells from me, because it isn't theft to steal from a ghost."

# 35

Why don't you like the light if you are blind?

I talk to you, why don't you talk to me?

Where did you come from?

I saw you washing. Why do you have all those scars? Did someone do something bad to you or did some kind of beast do that? Are there tigers where you are from?

Do you get lonely being alone? I get so lonely. But we aren't alone, are we?

You don't answer my questions. I wish you would.

# 36

She did not tell the girl she would follow. She simply slid into the cool water. She had never swum before, but she'd seen frogs and when she'd watch the girl, she looked much the same. Shortly before sunrise, the sky was the color of lead, the waves liquid charcoal. Unused to the water, she could not coordinate her breathing, but she swam her way off-shore, and in the clear water – black to anyone else – she could see the girl's pale shape down below. She felt like an eagle gliding over her young.

She could learn to hunt here as well as anywhere else. She was becoming a mother again. She could stay, could she not, every night singing the girl deeper in sleep so that whatever haunted her let her be? She could learn to dive herself, just another form of hunting. They could swim together.

Red flames. The vision of the Mantis with her son in his arms, cooing over him, licking his face, smashed behind her eyes, and the dark sea somehow flared red; not the sun. She could not stay.

Could she take the girl with her? She was barely able to survive here. In the mountains? Could she stay silent for days, stalking game? Could she weave watertight shoes from wicker, could she read signs of game, days old, in the forest loam, could she survive long enough to die if the Moongirl ever did find the demon? Can I take her to die?

Can I leave her here? She could survive, could she not? She did last winter. Why not another and another, this girl who was already outgrowing her clothes, with no skill at making her own, and no way to acquire them? Why could she not survive, this skinny child who already shivers in the summer waves, this girl living by the seashore who has not been found only because a man has not wandered down the cliffs?

This terrible thing.

Love.

# 37

"Girl, where's the boat?"

(?) "Obasan, why?"

"We are going fishing, out in the sea."

"But it's night? No one can fish at night without lights, and my people don't do that. We'll be lost. There's not even a moon."

"I will guide you."

"But you can't see."

"Only in the day. You are a girl of the sea? You can see in the water? I am a woman of the night. I cannot see in the day because the sun is cruel beyond measure, she is a goddess smiling on hell, and fire is just a child of the sun. There is only kindness in the dark. Let us go out to the sea. I can feel another autumn on its way. This winter will be hard. We must gather enough to last winter long. Get the boat."

The waves rock gently. The Moongirl watched the girl scull the boat with its long oar, and then silently pushed her aside, and imitated the same motion. She turned her head, sniffing the breeze, smelling the land behind her, listening for the faint sound of the waves upon the shore. The stars over the sea, grains of crystal cast up within the silent void. A harsh whisper, "There. Throw your net there."

"I cannot see a thing!"

"Throw your net there."

What does she see? The stars flicker on the surface of the sea, they stretch and puddle, merge and break apart, as if trying to achieve life and form, and there, under the surface, a ribbon of life, eyes a faint glow, moving lines of scales swirling arabesques beneath the waves. The net drops and the girl draws it in, the shards of silver coalescing into a single mass, a ball of life, heavy, struggling, onto the deck. No words to be said. Bonito. Massive as a woman's thigh: muscular, fighting, enough life for weeks.

Fins cut the surface. Night fishing. Sharks. Women. Life feeds life. The Moongirl prays. A shark rolls besides the boat. "You are the big one, here, yes? This is your forest." She reaches down and trails her hand along its harsh skin, and thinks of bears.

Three weeks pass. Every night fishing. In the daytime, the girl fillets and dries the bonito, some still full of oil for eating and the rest, hung over a slow fire so that all the fat drips out of them, leaving small wedges, hard as a brick to be shaved for broth.

"Obasan, we have enough. This is a winter's worth."

"No, not yet. We'll keep fishing."

Some nights, the girl glances at the other and sees, fleetingly, a faint smile on her lips. Other times, tears silently falling. Sometimes the woman whispers, raving scraps of words. The girl has learned not to ask. She has learned to leave another to her own grief and joy. Her mind quiets. She is not alone, no longer lightning's child. Just a girl.

# 38

"Come girl. One more night."

This night is different. The girl finds the wolf-dog sitting in the bow, ears up, looking attentively out to sea. In the floor of the boat are bundles, neatly tied, of dried bonito, and others of dried abalone, still others of shell, a backpack with the Moongirl's possessions, and another, newly made from bent willow saplings for the girl.

"Where are we going? This is everything we have."

"You will show me."

"What?"

"We are going to your home."

"NO! I can't!"

"We are going to your home. Listen to me, girl. There is a void in me. It will never be filled. There is another mother with such emptiness, because it doesn't matter who or what did the stealing, the void inside is the same. I will speak to your mother. You will not speak. If your people will not have you back, I will take you with me as long as I can, but I do not know how long that can be."

"I can't go back. I am a ghost to them! Take me with you. Why won't you just take me with you now?"

"Because I am going to hell, and I do not know if I and mine will be able to return. I do not know if I will want to return. But I know that even my hell is better than your life as a ghost back on that shore, so best you go back to your little paradise if we can. We'll decide what to do if they still think you a ghost. Hush. Just tell me where to aim."

# 39

Roll of muscles in the back. Naked. Smell of rich sweet air and salt, splash of a manta ray, flying fish whistling over the bow of the boat. Smell of girl. Stars singing like the flutes at the old shrines as the kannushi usher the gods back to their homes, an iodine breeze twining her limbs, up between her legs and sliding over her scars, sliding along each ridge of flesh and out over the ocean again. There to the right, schools of fish roll, massing in a ball, herded by sailfish, their huge dorsal fins flaring, slashing through the swirling orb, the waves rocking, rocking, faint blue lights on the waves, there, there, and over there, luminescent algae swishing and swirling, there, there, there, the oar creaking, roll of muscles in the back, sweat trickling down one cheek and neck.

Girl weeping.

Girl pointing.

The open sea.

The sun rising at their backs.

Moongirl unfurling her wings of hair, her raven wings, and wrapping them tightly across her eyes. On her head, a basketlike wicker hat, hiding most of her face.

"There. That way."

Over the horizon, voices, men laughing, the splash of water, the creak of oars. The girl reaches out, and caresses a clawed breast with her fingertips, weeps for the woman instead of herself. Moongirl rows on.

In the distance, the sound of whistling breaths. Men laughing; grunting with effort as they pull buckets of abalone and seaweed from the waves, as they pull women and rocks from the floor of the ocean.

She ceases to scull the boat, bends down and puts on a kimono, ties it tight, ties on sandals of hemp twine, and begins rowing again.

The boat pulling closer.

A single shout. Silence.

A girl's weeping. A girl's whispers. "Left. Pull left. Now right. The beach is ahead."

Children's voices laughing. Then silence.

A woman unloads heavy bundles on the beach. A year's worth of abalone. A winter's worth of bonito. A girl sits in a boat. Silent. The wolf-dog gets up from his place at the point of the bow, and delicately, on three legs, edges back, circles behind the girl. Lowering his muzzle, he lifts her arm and slides underneath it.

Moongirl walks up the rocky beach. She reaches out with her staff. The smell of the sea covers all. The village is silent. She wanders to-and-fro, learning the contours of the beach, learning the slope of the land, finding the edge where the village smells braid with those of the sea: cooking fires, the smell of millet (how long since she ate grain?), human beings, flesh and sweat.

The children on the beach have run away. The old women in the town stare from the outskirts. Those in the boats are pulling hard for the shore. One child, bolder, edges forward. Naked in the sun and unafraid of this strange sight, she edges close and says, "Obasan, can't you see anything."

"No child, not a single thing."

"What are you trying to find?"

"I want to find Iwaki-san."

"I can show you." And the child takes her hand, hers so warm, so soft, it almost breaks her. She once held such a hand. She convulses, tears whirling from her belly to her eyes to her mouth. She swallows her tears. Whispers.

"Wait.

Wait.

126

Live.

Wait."

"What, obasan? What did you say?"

"Nothing, child. Let us go to Iwaki-san."

By this time, the boats of the village landed, a flotilla of brawny men and sun-browned women. They stare at the dog in the boat and do not see the girl. Silently, gripping oars and pry-bars, they follow the woman who is following the child.

# 拳光

「Kenko」

# 40

"Iwaki-o-baa! Iwaki-o-baa! There's a lady without eyes to see you!"

Inside a bustle, an incredulous cry. "Asako! Are you up to your mischief again? What are you say . . . ."

A woman old beyond her years, sickened by something grating and hard, her face riven by loss, stands at the open veranda, and sees the whole village standing silently, staring, and there in front of her is something out of a dream. A naked little girl, the imp of their small village, hand-in-hand with a woman in a tattered kimono with the wicker hat of an itinerant mendicant, standing silently, leaning on a staff.

"By the gods, what . . . .?"

The woman let go of the child's hand, and it seemed like the most difficult thing imaginable, as if a ghost of her hand still holds that of the child, her whole posture one of grief. Voice catching, rasping, as if struggling its way out of a tangle of tree roots that pull it backwards under the earth: "Iwaki-san. I am a woman of the mountains, not the sea. I am a woman of the night, not the day. But I am a mother. You have three children, not two, one you lost and feared never found. I found her. She was lightning's child, so she said you said. That was untrue. Perhaps the lightning god possessed her for a time, but he doesn't own her now. I have brought her home to you. She has not sinned. The lightning in her sinned. I am a mother and I have lost my own as well. Perhaps I cannot save mine, but you can save yours.

Come to the sea with me, your daughter told me the sea hurt you grievously, but come, please come, see what the waters have returned to you."

"Girl," she whispered, "May I have your hand again? Take me to the sea."

The child and the mother began to walk through the silent staring folk and then, a sound of footsteps behind. Two mothers breathing heavily in the dust. Down to the sea they went.

They passed the bundles, and pointing with an open hand, the Moongirl said, "For the village. Your daughter's apology. And mine—for asking you to not live by the village rules. I once lived in a village, and rules are not always good to daughters."

She beckoned to the girl, who silently left the boat. People on the beach. Staring at the wolf-dog, who had seen such a thing as that? A blind woman and a wolf-dog?

"'Okaa. Okaa..." Girl weeping.

"Okachan."

The sun scalding down. The heat of the day. A village of silence. Who can see a ghost in the sunlight?

Cry of seabirds. People unmoving. Child weeping. Standing in the sun, the hours pass, the cruel sun burning, a ghost weeping, unseen in a village of silence.

A woman weeping. Arms opening as if they had never spread before, like old oak creaking, arms opening. A child runs in a mother's arms. Sisters run into a mother's arms, into a sister's arms. A father weeping. A village weeping.

Moongirl pushing out a boat into the waves, woman and dog blindly going out into the waves. When night falls, the stars will show her the way.

"Wait. Please wait. Stop her, please stop her." She keeps rowing. Three girls plunge into the sea, three sisters swimming for the boat. Two have no idea what they are chasing.

"Obasan. Don't go. Stay with me. Stay with us."

Moongirl kneels in the boat, reaches down and caresses her cheek. "No more waiting for me."

Rows on.

A pool of moonlight in the black sea.

# 41

Wandering again. She had to stay away from human habitation most of the time, so she washed in isolated streams, usually icy cold, then combed out her long hair with a few drops of camellia oil. She kept her clothes clean as well, and when they wore out, she stole strips of cloth from disassembled kimono, drying on poles to be resewn the next day. She didn't want to steal from the poor, so her clothes, pantaloons and jacket became a patchwork of different opulent fabrics. She would have appeared clownish, but out of sight, who was to see?

She was a wonderful huntress, and the dark was her home. With a spear, a snare or a matagi bow, she could take any prey, and with those terrible hands that the anma had bequeathed her, she could disassemble most men into constituent parts, were she to get hold of them.

But this would not be enough to save her son. She had to fight a demon. The only way to learn to fight death was to go to the realm of death; how else could she develop the skills to survive? For a woman, though, death was not that hard to find.

She stole a fine kimono, and after watching the whores at their trade, she walked the roads where men hunted, looking for women walking the roads. A road whore was as low as a woman could sink— either she had no protection, or she ended up with a pimp who ran her into the earth for a few coins until he threw her away, dying of disease or violence.

She set out to dance in the arms of death, but leave him walking. She learned to issue an invitation with an inclination of the head—how far she'd gone from her sweet matagi. She'd ignore the ordinary men: the drunk and lonely, who just wanted to sink into a pillow of warmth, who wanted to rock up against an alley wall, and forget who and what they were for just a few moments.

She waited for the one's who looked at her with disgust and contempt and kept on coming; the ones who smiled with cruelty; the one's in packs who wanted to shove something up each of her holes all at the same time, jackal grins on their faces as they locked eyes with each other, trying to tear through Her hair to bump the heads of their cocks in the middle of her. And most of all, she looked for armed men, the ones with daggers, sword-canes, and walking sticks.

She could mumble enough words to let them think they were going to get whatever they wanted, and she'd let them do—whatever—and when they were well on their way, she'd start to struggle, deliberately ineffectual, and they'd club her with a fist, or threaten her with a blade and here, too, she'd helplessly resist, or maybe spit in their face, and either way, it was serious now, and they'd start to take her apart. Their weapons were silver fangs, and just at the moment that they pierced her flesh, she'd somehow take one away, and she'd start to fight.

Sometimes she'd break free and if one had a staff, she'd use it just as the old woman had done. Eventually, she'd be in close, and with weapons flickering around her half-naked body, she having left her limbs deliberately tangled in the folds of her clothing to make things all the more difficult for herself, she'd leave the man or men unconscious on the ground. They had no permanent injuries—no broken bones. She would run the sharp edge of their own weapons along their veins and arteries, just parting the skin, sometimes even exposing blood vessels in their necks and wrists and groins, so that they throbbed and flinched in the cold air, so there would be no doubt that they were dead and dead and dead.

Sometimes she did this in daytime, learning to fight in the scalding light.

Once they were unconscious, she'd strip them naked, and strew their clothes around them. She'd stab their weapon in the ground, next to the artery in their neck. They'd awake and scuttle around, dressing themselves, wondering if that demon bitch

132

was still nearby, and some of them, at least, wondering if the next time they approached a woman that they might be hurt rather than she. She'd be long gone; once such an incident occurred she knew she'd have to leave town. She didn't expect these men to tell the authorities, but they might gather their friends and go on the hunt, in numbers too great to overcome, whether by day or night.

She didn't help other women by what she was doing. She probably made things worse. The men learned no lessons. They simply took out their shame on their wives, their daughters and other whores. She couldn't even conceive of that—she was dead to most of the world. The girl from the sea was gone; her boy was fully alive to her once more. Slowly, gradually, she drifted north-wards, and six long years after the demon shattered her life, she found herself back in Akita. Her home.

# 42

Kenko was walking towards the waterfall, about an hour before sunset, when he heard the voices over the roar of the water. Men shouting, with that gleeful bloodlust you'd only hear when they were about to hurt a woman. And something else, something not human, snarling with rage. He began to run. At the riverbank, on the other side below the falls, he saw a mass of six men, one with a short spear, the rest with swords or knives, yelling as they swaggeringly approached a woman and a wolfish three-legged dog. He was cut off by the river, and he didn't know how to swim. He could only wade across, water up to his neck, stumbling on the river rocks and moss. He didn't think he'd be in time.

The woman was dressed oddly, in a patchwork of fabric, bright and dark, sewn into the pantaloons and short coat you'd see on matagi, only men in his previous experience, and anyway, their clothes were dark, meant to blend in with the trees and rocks. She wore a wicker hat, covering half of her face. Off to the side were a staff and a pack-frame, which she'd set down at the approach of her pursuers. She reached into her jacket. The sun glinted off of steel—a matagi blade.

The men continued to approach as Kenko struggled through the fast flowing water. One of them began yelling. "You shit-stinking whore! You remember what you did to me back in Sakata? Left me naked in a ditch, slashed up my skin like a stencil maker, didn't you? And just because I was fucking drunk, huh? You must have had your pimp hit me from behind. You would have robbed me too, if you could have, huh? But too bad for you, I never carry money for whores. I don't give, bitch. I take.

You are going to suffer for what you did. Maybe I could have let it go. I've left enough of your sisters naked in alleys, so a little payback could be fair, I guess, but it was Kinebusa who found me. He drags me back to the boss, still naked. Wouldn't even let me get my clothes. I had to give up a finger to apologize for shaming the gang. You fucking cunt! I had to cut off my finger for you! You think you can mess with Maeda of the Tostuka-gumi? We've been on your trail for months now, ever since my hand healed. We'll cut you to pieces."

Looking directly at the screaming man with the spear, she pulled off her jacket and under-jacket. Below that she was naked. The men stopped, stunned by what they saw. Breasts without nipples, and a web of thick scars, carved in her body. She slowly turned her back to show the white and red ridges crawling down to her buttocks, and slashing up and over her shoulders. She turned again, where they twined round her to rip down towards her waistband, surely continuing further into her groin. Somehow, they held a design like a tree, with shapes that suggested something trapped within the branches.

She then took off her wicker hat and cast it aside, and the men unconsciously flinched, mouths agape, whispering, "That's just wrong. What is that? Maeda—you tried to fuck that? *Obake da*, a monster!" Her hair was bound over her eyes, but not mere wings. She now wove it in an intricate lattice, for since she'd left the girl, she had learned to fashion it in a kind of layered screen that admitted only as much light as she could stand. She learned to keep her face turned away from any direct contact with the sun, her head moving in an almost perpetual dance of avoidance as she slid sidelong through the blaze of day. With her eyes so bound, her day-world was a pointillist cloud of glowing particles, beautiful and vicious, flaring in small explosions of agony whenever light reflected from a drop of water or a patch of snow. Within this rainbow haze, objects, be they trees or men, coalesced into ill-defined shapes when they came close.

The agonizing flash of light on a weapon provoked reactions as fast as yours might be were you to touch a burning coal. To watch her stalk and kill a boar in the daytime was to see a miracle, tracking his rough shape within a swirl of ever changing mote and hue, her body lithe as a panther, her head moving independently, as if another being entirely, bobbing and dancing away from the cruel sun, shifting senses from hearing to sight to scent.

The woman's face, what could be seen, was lined with grief, as if to say, "What can you do to me?" and she held up an arm and simply pointed in the direction that they had come, her wolf-dog still snarling. She murmured something, and the animal became silent, sat down and simply watched.

They milled around, muttering, but they would not leave. Maeda started screaming, "What are you waiting for, so she looks like a monster, fuck her scars, she's still a whore, I want to see her guts looped on the point of my spear!"

Kenko was hauling himself up the steep bank of the river, just in time to see them attack. She retreated, and the men shifted from momentary confusion to confidence at her withdrawal. She moved backwards as they pursued, and she suddenly turned a 'hook,' almost doubling back on them. The sharp unexpected curve led the men to line up like fish on a string. The man with the spear rushed in, intending to stab her in the belly. She could live a long time that way; in fact, he could nail her to the ground like a butterfly, while the others did whatever they wanted.

Except he was dead. First in, first down. As he stepped into the ideal range, she was still withdrawing, and she suddenly shifted, sliding to one side, as his spearhead flared agonizing fire amidst the dark mass he created within a multi-hued cloud of light. He didn't even perceive the knife thrusting deep into his throat

She slashed sideways and caught the next man at the waist, cutting open his belly, and dropping to one knee, thrust the blade between another's legs, and ripped completely through the femoral artery, the spray of blood suffusing her world in a crimson mist.

A fourth grabbed at her from behind, only to have the snarling wolf-dog leap over her head and onto his chest, closing his jaws on his face. As he fell backwards, the beast shifted his grip and tore out his throat. One of the two remaining men saw a chance and attacked from the side, just as she was regaining her feet. She stepped backwards and blocked low, cutting his wrist, then thrust upwards into his bladder. Kenko was running towards the melee when things got even more bizarre. The woman, her face expressionless, walked towards the remaining man, opening her arms as if to embrace him.

He charged. All he could see in front of him was a mass of scarred flesh, covered with his friends' blood, surmounted by a round eyeless face. All he could see in his mind's-eye was his sword slashing her in two.

Kenko, still running, gasped yet again. She waited until it was unnecessarily, impossibly late. The sword blade seemingly touching her hair, she somehow twisted to the side. She rammed her blade over his descending arms, and up into his body, the track of the blade like a dragon flipping its tail as it dove. She was not unscathed, however—the blade slashed deeply into one breast.

He slowed down, walking cautiously towards her on the blood-spattered ground: four dead men, two dying poorly, weeping and screaming, one trying desperately to stuff his bowels back in his belly, the other wrapped in a ball around himself.

The wolf-dog sprang to his feet, snarling deep in his throat, and she whirled in a crouch, holding her knife blade low at her side.

He stopped and held up a hand, his short sword still sheathed in his belt. "I'm not them. I knew what they were when I heard their voices. I have no idea what you are or what has happened to you, but I know what they are. I knew I wasn't going to be able to save you in time, but I was going to do right by you afterwards. Obviously, I wasn't needed. You are brilliant, but I wonder why you deliberately flirt with death, why you have done that to your eyes, and why you don't kill simply your enemies quickly. Is it a game to you, or are you trying to learn something?"

Splattered with gouts of the men's blood, her own pulsed slowly from the wound in her breast, flowing along her scars. She stared in his direction, trying to discern him within the glittering sparks of her day-world, her lips trembling as she tried to speak.

"Go to the river," he said. "Wash the blood off yourself. You'll need to tend to your wound—or someone will—but not polluted by their blood. It's the middle of nowhere here, but the bodies still have to be disposed of. Not too many people come by, but there is always a chance. There's a split in the rocks up that little valley. It's deep and there's no reason for anyone to walk back that way. Go to the river. I will dispose of them."

She nodded. First, she wiped her blade on one man's jacket. She would not let the blade rust. Before her own body, she would clean the blade.

# 43

Woman and wolf-dog went around a bend in the river. There was the waterfall, cascading over the rocks, an arc of white shot with green, a jumble of boulders on either side. She knelt beside the water's edge, drops of blood falling from her breast, crimson flowers dissolving in the foam. She carefully washed her knife, removing as much water as she could by cutting through the air, the blade whistling with each slash. Taking out a strip of cloth from her bundle, she wiped it dry, and then from a small pouch, removed a container with clove-scented oil, which she carefully wiped on the blade. Finally, she replaced it in its sheath. A moment later, the sun set. The night rolled across the cedars like a silent wave. She unbound her hair, tied it once at the neck and let it fall over her shoulders, her eyes once again caressed by the gentle fingers of darkness.

She could still hear the cries of agony from the two surviving men. She had not, by any means, lost the capacity to care about other's pain, but this did not extend to murderers and rapists. She stepped back around the bend, however, because she wanted to see, for sure, what the big man was doing. Squatting some distance away to avoid the loops of his guts, he was talking to the disemboweled man, whose black blood pooled on the ground.

She knew his voice. Several years since she had so briefly passed him in the brothel entrance, he was still a big man, leaner now, pared down by the battering waters of the cataract, with grizzled close-cropped hair. The wounded man obviously was begging for something, but Kenko merely sighed. He got up, walked up to the man, who continued to clutch at the billows of his intestines as they spilled out of the gaping lips of the wound. Kenko squatted down again, and drew a knife from behind his hip. Hiding it from the man's sight, he put a massive hand over his eyes, then quickly and cleanly, cut the carotid artery on the side opposite to him. The blood spurted in an arc of ebony, then guttered onto the ashen colored ground. The man kicked and flopped, one hand reaching for his neck, back to his guts, and then he was still.

He then went over to the other man, scarcely more than a boy, who was begging for the day to begin again, for this to be a dream, cursing his friends, cursing the woman, cursing his mother for birthing him. He would die, too, but it would take a long time, as his ruptured bladder would rot him from the inside out. The big man spoke again. His voice suddenly whip-cracked loudly, and the youth stopped howling. He seemed to be trying to speak, reaching out a hand in supplication. The big man took the hand and pulled, which rolled his body so that it faced away. Again, he cut his throat.

He let him drop and went over to one of the other bodies that had already bled out. He stripped off his kimono so that he was nearly naked. Despite his nearly seventy years, he was massively built, with more than a few scars. He heaved the body onto his shoulder, some black blood tracing down his back which gleamed in the twilight, luminescent, and walked off towards the crevasse he had mentioned to her. Satisfied that he was keeping his word, she again walked around the bend, quickly stripped off her clothes, and washed herself clean of the polluting blood. Still naked, she washed out her clothes and wrung them to mere dampness. Then she bound her chest with a clean cloth, but it soon became soaked with blood, the wound too deep to stop with mere pressure. She took a second, well-worn set of clothes, similar to the first, and put on the pantaloons, and sandals. She put everything else back in her bundle, and carrying it and her weapon in one hand, her clean jacket in the other, she again came around the bend. The bodies were gone. The big man was gathering all the weapons together. He wanted no evidence of what happened, and so he tied the swords and spear together and carried them off to the crevasse. When he returned, he saw that she had kicked dirt over the bloodstains, and was now using a leafy branch to smooth down the earth and sand. Nothing had happened here.

Kenko was filthy: covered in sweat, blood, and other fluids from the dead men. He was angry, too, although he could not articulate why. The men were dead—and he was sure they deserved it—but he had no purifying sense of victory. All he'd done was clean up. He looked hard at the woman, still half naked, with her bizarre mutilated upper body, and bound and bleeding breast. She bowed to him, as if to say thank you and take her leave.

Kenko shook his head. "That's not right. Having cleaned up after you, and getting myself covered in the blood and filth of your . . . " he paused and raised an ironic eyebrow that was lost on her ". . .followers, I think I am owed, if not an explanation, at least your company for a meal. Anyway, that wound of yours needs to be sewn up. I can see from your clothes you are handy with a needle and thread. Maybe you can do it by yourself, but maybe not. It's something I can do if you cannot. I'm going to wash. I would be grateful if you waited for me here."

# 44

She followed him silently through the woods, up a side-gulley that cut into a cliff. Because of its angle, it was only visible when coming down the main valley, something no one did, because beyond, there were just mountains followed by more mountains. They entered his dwelling, and he stirred the coals back into flame, and boiled some water in a black iron kettle. As he lit the fire, she flinched and quickly bound her eyes with her hair. He made no comment.

"I got interested in wounds, having had more than a few. So when anyone was cut or stabbed, I watched how their wound was treated and how it healed. I noticed that if anything was dirty—the needle, the thread, the wound, the skin, or the hands of the person sewing—the wound festered. So I keep things clean. There are no guarantees, though, because if the bone is even scratched, things seem to rot. That one looks like it's gone down to the ribs." He poured the boiling water into a basin, and after it had slightly cooled, washed his hands. He got up, threw out the water, poured in some more and said, "I would be quite happy to take care of your wound. I'm sure you would do a per-fectly adequate job, but the angle is awkward. If you please."

She silently took off the makeshift bandage, and the wound, a red mouth, still seeped blood. He was right; he could see bone underneath. He made no comment on her scars—that this was her story to tell only if she chose.

She was leaning forward, her breasts hanging, rosy pink yet horribly scarred, like apples clawed by winter's talons. "This will hurt—a lot. We cannot sew anything into your flesh, not the slightest speck." With a small cedar cup, he carefully poured the scalding water over the wound. Water and clots of blood dripped onto a mat of grass that he'd put in front of her. He carefully inspected inside the wound, separating it with his fingers. Over and over again, he poured water into the bleeding flesh. She shook, her lips trembling, but although nearly white with pain, she made neither sound nor movement. Finally, satisfied that he had washed out any dirt or grease from the man's sword, he had her hold her flesh together with a clean cloth, cupping her breast with both hands like the most tender of fruit. He put the kettle back on the flame, dropping in needle and thread. Pulling them from the water, he began to sew.

"I've gotten quite good with needle and thread. See? All these clothes are mine. I taught myself. I'll match my stitches against any woman. If I sew this well, with small, tight stitches, there'll hardly be a sca . . ." Still sewing, he stopped his prattle at the absurdity of what he was about to say; her flesh was as corrugated as one of those temple gardens, raked into patterns to mimic the waves of the sea.

# 45

She was shaking with fatigue and shock. He more or less forced her to eat a rice ball, but she continued to shiver. "It's dark, it's cold, and you need rest. Go ahead and sleep in my bedding."

She sensed no harm in the man, but she had to make things clear. Placing a hand near her dagger, she said, "I sleep alone. I had a man. I was perfect in him, and he in me. That's finished now."

He smiled wistfully. "I have had more women than I can count. It was never perfect, and neither was I. It's finished for me too. Sleep. It's warm enough for me over here."

# 46

There were few, if any wolves left in Japan. The Japanese wolf was small, only a little bigger than a coyote or jackal, and they were actually revered in many shrines as protectors of crops. Her wolf-dog had found her, he had stayed with her beside the sea, eating fish and shellfish for months, followed her during her wanderings and her insane attempts to train herself by courting murder and rape.

They were almost home now; only a few hundred miles to the north lay the place where he was born. He was wont to run out at night—he came and went as he pleased. His bond to her was like a comet round the sun; he might be gone for days, hunting or finding a mate, she never knew, but he always returned.

He had watched them enter Kenko's hut. He gazed at it, seeing the fire-glow through cracks in the wall, but the warmth did not tempt him. The air around was too rich with smells, both new and familiar, and suddenly he turned and began to run due north.

# 47

Despite all he had done, her flesh swelled and purpled, and she burned and she raved. He slashed the stitches that were almost buried in her swollen breast, and then jerked backwards from the jet of blood and pus that was released. And still she raved.

Some poets describe a human life as a stream, flowing from a small droplet at birth, winding its way gently in childhood, then tumultuously over rocks and cliffs in youth, to achieve stately maturity as a river until it wends it way into the sea. But this was pandemonium, splattering here and there from past to further past, to future and back again: a thrill of a nerve behind a thigh when a tongue traced its way slowly up from the knee, an ice cave full of laughter, a fire, a harsh and cold mother's hand, another dog, now dead, a husband now dead, a child, a baby, a child, a boy, a child, a boy in the reeking claws of a Mantis, a spray of blood and fingers, the crying of a bear-cub whose mother had just been killed, a mumbling, muttering bumblebee, an ice cold river and a second birth, a young girl emerging from the sea, a lullaby, a soft cheek, a baby nuzzling an unscarred breast, a monkey clutching its belly with an arrow blossoming right in its center, screaming as it falls from a tree into the snow, a tiny naked girl on a beach holding a hand, an ice cave glowing gold in oil-lamp's fire, the sea at night, lit luminescent midst grey and black, a mountain ledge that crumbles beneath ones feet into an avalanche that screams, then moans its way down a narrow valley, the light that blinds, a lovely laughing man, a malevolent, gleeful torturous egg emerging from a ceiling, spiraling down into a small chamber filled with happiness, carving and cutting and slashing, a hell of light, hell of night, the man-hell, where women are ripped and raped and rent, and now she's dying, an ice cave, a child, a monster and pain beyond pain beyond loss beyond pain.

By the fourth day, her raving had softened to whispers, something different: "*Kani don, kani don, doko iku no?*" *Saru no bamba e, adauchi ni.*" This he knew, because his mother used to tell him the same. A child's story.

"Mrs. Crab, Mrs. Crab. Where are you going?"

"I'm going to the monkey's place, to take my revenge."

Over and over she told the story, as if to a child who couldn't hear it enough. He remembered how he, too, would beg his mother to tell it once again as she took on the voices of all the crab's helpers.

He had thought that her screaming was pure insanity, but he remembered, while working further south a number of years ago, a pathetic little fellow whom the brothel used to clean out the rooms. He was shattered, a terrified mouse. Kenko asked him what had happened to make him so scared, and he mumbled, "The Mantis took my wife. He took her from my arms and I didn't even wake." One of the other yojimbo told him that the mountain folk had this legend about a monster, neither insect nor man. "They say he used to steal women, but he got old and he now steals kids. Ahh, it's just talk. Where I come from, it's *karasu-tengu*, the crow goblins, and Hatano, over there, used to hear about *kappa*—you know, the ones that live in rivers and have bowls in the top of their head that they have to keep filled with water, or they'll die? Same stuff, I guess."

Since he'd arrived in Akita, though, he'd heard more stories of the Mantis: of murders and rapes and children stolen. He had supposed that the mountain folk needed a demon to explain the normal tragedies of daily existence. Her too? Maybe she was mad. She heard the stories, and attached it to some miscarried child, or one lost to childhood illness, all too common. But the scars! They were carved with purpose, almost artistry, by someone of almost preternatural skill. Savage slashes they were, but none to vital areas, as if he outlined every place of death on her body and either cut around it or over it, too shallow to find its mark. He cast his mind about, recalling stories he heard over the past couple of years—a murder here or there, a village burned. No lost children, but a few strange tales that he'd brushed aside. Come to think of it, the stories had changed, because over the last couple years he'd heard of two Mantis: large and small.

# Murder

A man walks down a forest path. He bears two swords on his belt. He has killed several men in duels. Living far in the country, he has ignored the recent edicts from the central government to disarm and live in modern times. A child darts out from the bushes, and snatches the shorter of his two blades. The man feels nothing. He only realizes what has happened when a pebble strikes the back of his head, and he turns and sees his short sword in the child's hand. Outraged, he demands the return of his weapon. The child takes a stance, pointing the weapon at his eyes. He whips out his long sword, intending to split the boy in two. He is known for cutting chopsticks thrown near him, a feat that has won him fame. The boy is not cut in two. He is standing somewhere else. After a number of slashes, the boy begins to cut the man's clothes from his body, leaving him unscathed. The child is so fast that the man does not dare lower his blade or his hand to untangle himself, and soon he is nearly naked, his feet tangled in the cloth. The boy calmly walks forward, the short sword lowered, and the samurai, centering himself over his bound feet, makes a perfect cut from collarbone to hip. The child bends backwards so that the blade runs along his body, shivering his flesh to accommodate the quicksilver curve of the blade. He coils low to the ground, then upwards again, ramming the blade through the base of the man, then twists, a half-turn, coring him like an apple. The man's mouth and eyes, three round 'o's of shock, he dies a hero, not making a sound. The boy does not know what a hero is.

# 48

She would not die. He laid her wound open again and cleaned it out. Eventually, he cauterized it, the most horrible thing he'd ever seen or done. For the rest of his life, the smell of burning flesh haunted his dreams, as did her eyes, absent, staring through and beyond him. She saw someone else, someone awful beyond measure and she whispered, "You will not make me weep again. I have cried all my tears. I am coming for you, and bringing him home."

He did not dare risk sewing her together again. Instead, he covered the wound in spider webs, and so it began to knit, scabbing over, brittle and thick, purplish-red on her pale skin. On the ninth day, she opened her eyes and gazed around her. By holding a skein of hair over her eyes, she made it just dim enough to be bearable. Kenko was sitting nearby, dozing, and the sun, through the smoke hole, sent down a single shaft of light that illuminated the dusty air, burning like tiny birds of fire.

She lay quietly, watching him sleep. She could see the kindness in him, the massive gentility, like an old cedar tree. She tried to rise and moaned in pain, thankfully falling back before she managed to tear open her wound again.

He woke immediately, and quickly moved, one massive hand holding her in place.

"Where is my friend?"

"Your friend?"

"My wolf, my dog, my only friend."

"He followed us up to the hut, but I haven't seen him since."

She almost sobbed, her hand groping the air for that familiar shape, the last thing she had of her former life.

"You must not move. You have to gain strength if you want to fight him."

She started. "Shhh. Don't even try to talk yet. I thought he was just a legend, just another story to scare the children. You spoke during your . . .sleep. I have enough of an idea of what he is and what he's done. I must tell you something, though. I watched you fight. You are brilliant, the best woman I've ever seen, and among men, only a few surpass you. But I've seen what he did to you. You cannot beat him, not with what you have."

Her eyes flamed. Again, he held up a hand. "There's one thing you don't know. Just one thing. I know you were testing yourself at the edge of possibility, but you got cut. That's the proof that you do not have enough. The thing you are hunting is beyond the edge of possibility. And from what I hear, he is not alone. So rest. There is one thing you need to know, and I can teach it to you."

# 49

He left. He returned. He cleaned the hut. He cooked. She slept in the day. She avoided the firelight. Finally, he asked why she did the weird thing with her hair. "The sun hates my eyes, and all of her children do too."

She got out of bed, and began taking short walks. She cleaned the hut. She gathered wood. She cooked. They didn't speak. What would they talk about? The weather? Murder? Monsters?

The scab dropped off the wound, leaving flesh, purple and fragile. She massaged the skin with oil, the same oil she used to protect her blade. Smelling of cloves, she started stretching, harmonizing her movements with her breath.

He beckoned with his head, and she followed him in the forest. He took two stout tree limbs, and gave one to her. She did what he did, striking the trees, her body relaxed, the sound resounding from the heart of the tree. He hung a log from a tree branch and set it a-spinning, hissing viciously through the air. She'd block or cut it, but if she didn't strike it perfectly, it would whip around, slashing towards her face. After a week, he took some small metal skewers from the hearth that he used to place small whole fish at the edge of the fire to cook, and stuck them in the ends of the logs. Now, she'd deliberately strike the log off-center, the slender metal spikes, crusted with black burnt oils, spinning, slashing towards her eyes. She'd cut it again and again and again, calculating where it would oscillate next, moves ahead, sometimes swaying, judging its path by the whistle of air from the tips of the skewers. Then he hung a second log, the two of them clashing as they spun and collided. She was knocked unconscious and once, a skewer went right through her cheek. She stood there silently, the tree limb growing from her face. She eased it out and silently went back to the river, and washed her face and her mouth, until the blood tasted clean, with no taint of soot or fish. Then back again, day after day, until the two, then three, then four spinning spiked enemies whirled around. To an observer, it was as if she passed through them, a chaotic, clonking, mess, then as she refined things further, they whirled and hummed like wasps, never touching each other or her.

Having seen her matagi blade, he carved wooden knives and a short spear. They began to train together, he using any object or weapon that came into his reach. Eventually, they shifted to steel. He taught her nothing; he simply attacked her and let her respond as best she could. Bit by bit, he introduced her to all of his skills, sometimes within the swirl of near combat, sometimes slowly, taking it apart so she could perceive it. She did not learn to do what he did; she learned how to respond to whatever he did. He fought her at every range. He grappled her, using his superior strength and then his superior skill; he threw dirt in her face and a dagger suddenly at her foot. She fought him with her spear and suddenly, separating it and throwing aside the shaft, fought him with her matagi blade. He disarmed her, but twisting like an eel whipping out of a cauldron, she slid free and attacked his body with her frightening hands. As she dropped to the ground, he deliberately attacked her breast with a knee, trying to grind it into her barely healed flesh, a wound that would have crippled her forever, and she folded into him, taking the knee on her ribs and drawing a hidden dagger, almost hamstrung him.

He gave her everything he knew, and taught her how to defeat it all. He learned everything she had and broke it to pieces, then taught her how to win anyway. She became his equal and then she surpassed him, the leopard greater than the tiger, the fox a mortal danger to the wolf.

One night, they trained hours long, and perhaps seven out of ten bouts, she defeated him. Knowing the full measure of the man, she felt a wild hope that she was ready. She was faster than he, and could see in the dark.

"Once more?" He asked. She nodded. His blade was at her neck. She hadn't perceived a thing.

"Once more?" and he was on her, dropping her into the bamboo-grass, she instantly drawing her blade—too late. She could not feel him; he was like a cloud, her weapon pinned, the blood supply cut from her brain. Blackness.

"Once more?" The blade at her neck.

"Once more?" The blade at her neck.

"Once more?" Blackness.

"Once more?" Her clothes pulled around her head, blinding her, she was thrown into the gully at her back.

As she climbed back up the slope, "Once more?" He cut her this time, a shallow gash down her thigh.

"Once more?" She, streaked with blood, black in the moonlight. He unscathed.

"Once more?"

"Once more?"

"Once more?"

When the dawn chased the moon from the sky, her mind was close to shattering. As wild and deranged as the days after the murder, she began to shriek and could not stop.

Kenko slipped past her defenses one last time, disarmed her and wrapped her close to his massive chest. She sobbed, and achingly, tried to push herself free. He released her, and she crawled to her dagger, intending to cut her throat.

His scream of fury was like a serrated fang and she froze, her blade at her neck. He was enraged, truly enraged. "I showed you! An entire night I showed you what you need to know! Kill yourself then! Better that than let your son watch him flay you a second time! Do you want to stay the moon, only able to reflect and never to shine!!!? You make your own light or you die!" He heaved himself up and walked towards the waterfall. He ripped off his clothes and stood underneath the pounding water, almost driven to his knees. When he emerged she was quietly sitting on a rock beside the river, hair tied over her eyes.

# 50

He waded through the shallows, the water beading on his shoulders. Walking past her, his eyes warmed, glad and perhaps a little surprised that she was still alive. He picked up his kimono, and walked around the bend. He stripped off his loincloth, just a strip of muslin, really, and after wringing out the water, put it back on. He took the rest of his clothes back to a clearing and hung them so that the sun would bake out his sweat and her tears.

Once he was gone, she stripped off her own clothes, washed them on the rocks and spread them in the sun. She entered the water—almost as cold as her baptism at the hands of the old woman—and worked her way to the waterfall. She wasn't strong enough to stand underneath it at the center, but she picked a spot off to the side and ducked underneath, only to be smashed to the rocks. Spat out into the shallows, she worked her way back and this time, centering herself, stood there and let the water pound onto the top of her head and shoulders, the impact driving all thought from her brain. Her hair, unbound, whipped by the water, wrapped and unwrapped around her body. With her eyes squinted nearly shut, all she could see was foam. She moved further underneath the lip of rock, and found herself in a small chamber enclosed by rock and water. She yelled and the sound, amplified, rang like a temple gong, vibrating back and forth. She started chanting and yelling, then singing, her voice warped in waves, modulated by the shifting wall of water at her front. For the first time in years, she let everything go, madness and sanity both, and sang amidst the roar of the falls, the curtain of water a random factor, twisting and bending the tones. She laughed, and then ebbed to silence. The only sound was the water—a shifting whoop all around.

156

# 51

That evening, the only light a few glowing coals, he served her tea. Just as she took it, the point of his knife was at her throat. "What did you see?"

"Nothing. Just you serving me tea."

"Do it to me."

She couldn't. As she approached him to serve the tea, he drew away. Time after time, he moved before she could. Sometimes, he drew his blade. Once he knocked the tea away, spilling it on the ground. Sometimes, he drew his knife as she was whisking the tea. "You are telling me what you intend to do. You have to intend to serve me tea. Only that."

"How can I do that?"

<A raised eyebrow>

After several days, she retreated into herself. She felt no anguish or pain other than the constant ache and fear for her child. She longed for her wolf-dog who would sit with her while she puzzled out how to live. She curved her hand and stroked the air where he would be, but absent, this only brought back the void. So she went back to the waterfall, letting it batter her to exhaustion, and then she sat in the chamber of water, thinking nothing

Otherwise, they did not practice together. Instead, she arose and she trained herself. She found a trailing willow tree, and spent the days slipping and twining among its branches, her blade paring a single leaf from each willow switch.

Several weeks later, she was preparing some soup. Their custom was to keep the cooking fire outside, and bring in the coals later for warmth, so that she could keep her eyes unbound in the dim room. She thought with gratitude at all this man had done for her, and as she stirred the miso into the hot water, her heart grew tender. She entered the hut, smiling, a moment of peace between them and suddenly threw the lacquered bowl of hot soup right in his face, and her knife followed, the tip piercing his neck.

She stepped back, shaking. Bleeding and almost blinded by the hot soup, he staggered out of the hut to the stream of water that ran nearby and plunged his scalded face into the cool water. After a time, he returned. She was sitting quietly, near the coals, pale with shock at what had emerged from her. His face was red, and there were a few angry blisters along one cheek.

He laughed. "OK, you got it. Let's not do it that way again. Now, you will have to learn to do this while fighting. What he sees must never be what you are, and that will only work if what you show him is utterly true."

"But I hate."

"You cannot hide what you are, but there is always more of you. When we train, you are sometimes scared or angry, and sometimes you are full of joy and power, and sometimes you and I have moments of *mushin*, a mutual emptiness where the only thing matters is that perfect act. Unlike what the sword-saints tell you, though, mushin is not enough. Perfection leaves a trail, just like any other state of being. You cannot leave a trail. You must learn to hide within the truth, just as you did before you nearly burned my face off." He started laughing again, and after a moment, she did too, her first in six long years. She dipped a rag in a small bucket of water, and reached out to touch his face. He recoiled in mock horror, "No, not again. A truce, please, be nice to me tonight. We'll train tomorrow." She laughingly demurred and reached out further and he, laughing still, grabbed her wrist and yanked her right towards his massive fist. She did not resist. Instead she dove right into his pull, her face about to be crushed like an egg-shell. Her power augmenting his, she shifted his balance, and as he tilted ever so slightly, she was underneath his punch, and then outside his arm, with her blade gouging into the flesh above his liver. One push, and although he still might kill her, he would surely die in the process.

He had not stopped laughing throughout his attack. He released her wrist, and she drew back. Looking deeply into her eyes, he sat silently, as she gazed back at him. "Actually, there's no need to practice anymore." Reaching behind his back, he took a small knife, sheathed in lacquer, and handed it to her with a bow: "You may find this of use."

He did not love her. There was no space inside her for anything but the void of her loss. Nonetheless, here he sat more knowing of this woman than any in his life. A memory came to him, he still a youth with his young wife. They had left the village early one morning, climbed one of the hills in the surrounding area. They found a small clearing filled with mountain flowers, the bees buzzing, drunk on nectar, and they fucked, she on her hands and knees, he behind, riding her like a stallion on a mare. Afterwards, they lay on their tangled clothes, and green-and-black swallowtails, attracted by their sweat, landed on them, sipping the juice from their bodies. Their feet and tongues tickled, and they could feel the faint breeze of the fanning of their wings. It was almost frightening, almost too much to bear, and one or the other would twitch, and the butterflies would rise in a cloud of emerald and midnight, then alight again. Now, a lifetime later, he remembered her eyes, she utterly delighted in him, showing him everything, and he, utterly delighted in himself as well. What a wonderful day, what a terrible loss.

Here, near the end of his life, he truly saw a woman for the first time. She was a torn and haunted thing—he owed this moment between them to horror and violation, and a knife at his flesh. But he truly saw her, not himself in her at all. And she? She felt gratitude, more than she could possibly express, but she saw through him already. All she could see was beyond. He was merely a path, not a man.

He got up from the mats, gathered a few things for a trip back to town, and walked out the door. As he did, he reached down and with one finger, gentle as a butterfly's wing, touched her shoulder.

# Mother and Child

*A mother sleeps with a baby in her arms, scarcely three months old. There is a boy beside their futon. He cuts the baby's throat. She wakes with the dawn.*

# 狼
「Okami」

# 52

Why did he run away? He was as bonded to her as she was to him. They were a pack of two, and she was alpha. Why did he run when she was so sorely wounded? Why are you asking me? How do you expect me to know the mind of a wolf-dog? Am I a god? All I know is that he ran, and that he had been here before.

He moved through the woods, taking prey as he went, going up mountain passes, and sometimes turning around when he met a wall or a snowline. He skirted vermin-ridden villages and isolated farmhouses, crammed with mangy children, the women mostly bare-breasted, and the men, outside of winter, clad only in a loincloth and a hat. They huddled inside after dark, afraid of ghosts and goblins and Mantis alike.

The forests were mostly pine, but there were also birch, miles of white trunks, stippled with black, the bark peeling in sheets. He meandered here and there, going ever north, and after some weeks, he heard a faint sound, a rattling, waxing and waning with the wind. Like all carnivores, he was curious about new things. As he got closer, a smell came to him, a rank stench he knew well. Dogs do not hate smells for themselves—they roll in excrement and shove their snouts in carrion—the expression 'shit-eating grin' refers to you, Mr. Canis Lupus Familiaris. But they can hate a smell for what it means.

He bared his teeth, and lowered his head to the earth, the scent trail more direct than the sound of rattling bones on the wind. Creeping slowly upwards, hackles raised, he came to a cliff and, twenty feet below, a ledge and a tree, adorned with finger-bones, thousands in all. Were he to have gazed further, many hundreds of feet down, he might have seen shattered skulls, ribs, and cracked femurs, many fire-charred, and tattered cloth, the remnants of articles of clothing, large and small. He was a dog and a wolf, and the edge of cliffs held no fascination, neither for the depth or the view, and once he'd seen the rattling tree—not threat, not food—it was no longer of any interest whatsoever.

The smell, however, was another thing. The scent trail continued over the ridge and descending downwards, a winding narrow trail that hugged the mountainside, and the scent, this way, was two—for he could smell the boy as well.

Three more weeks north he went. Coming to a break in the trees, he could see a small fire. Seated beside the blaze were the Mantis and the boy. The wolf-dog knew him instantly, his pack-mate. He bunched his muscles, ready to spring in attack, to kill the beast that had killed his own, and then he stopped. It was not the boy! It was the boy's body, nearly six years grown, and the boy's smell, but not his smell. Twined within the boy's scent, once the happiest of odors, all well-being and joy, he smelled fear and rage, he smelled terror, he smelled cruelty. He smelled much like the Mantis. The wolf-dog has once been attacked by a rabid fox, scarcely half his size, foaming at the mouth, so ferocious that he retreated in fear, the only thing he had ever run from in his entire life. The boy smelled diseased in the same way.

Involuntarily, he whined, and two heads, man and boy, instantaneously lifted, scanning the woods. The boy picked up a smooth pebble, and without windup or forethought, threw it exactly where the sound had emanated, 50 yards distant. Had the wolf-dog not shied away, just as the sound slipped from his throat, his skull would have been shattered.

From that day on, a master stalked the masters. He nearly starved, because he would only leave them to hunt when they were occupied or asleep. The boy's training continued, more ferociously than before, but it was now "do what you wilt," rather than "do this." Carnage was not their daily fare; in a strange way, the Mantis was at something of a loss. He had his son. What were they to do? Most of his life had been a search for a child of his own, and now he had him. He knew, dimly, that too many human deaths would bring attention that not even he could survive. He'd even been through one of the larger towns late one night, and seen soldiers, bivouacked with guns. He stole a rifle and studied it: death at a distance, nothing he wanted for himself, but good to know.

All the same, carnage tasted so sweet, as did the tears of those bereft and ripped and soon to die. His tree, three centuries of agony festooned, craved decoration. What were they to do?

While he decided, they lived off the land and mostly hunted the most difficult of prey. The boy never spoke, never responded with any emotion that the Mantis could see; he simply gazed at him with luminous eyes and complied with whatever he was told.

He spotted a *momonga*, a flying squirrel, and they tracked it for some time. The boy had to kill it with his bare hands and teeth, and the gliding agile little beast kept eluding them. It would have been an easy kill had they worked in tandem, but this task was the boy's alone. Each time he spotted her, each tree he climbed, creeping up the trunk in increments so small that it seemed moss would outrace him, he got ever closer before she glided away.

During their wanderings, they came upon a woodcutter, he almost naked in the hot summer heat. Abandoning the squirrel, the boy crept behind the man, and as he stood, legs aspraddle, singing and pissing in the leaves, he slit his testicles with an obsidian flake. As the balls dropped from the rent sack, he ripped them from their white tethers and was gone, the man arched on his toes, screaming in shock, cupping the gushing blood at the root of himself. Unseen, the Mantises watched the man as he collapsed in a fetal curl, shrieking in bewildered pain. The boy handed one ball to his father, and they each popped theirs into their mouths, chewing and savoring the tough flesh. The Mantis grinned in pleasure, both at the taste and at his son. This was the first time he had done something on his own initiative. He stroked his hair as one does a cat. The boy, expression unchanged, gazed at the whimpering, bloodied man, turned to resume his hunt for the momonga.

Once they were gone, the wolf-dog approached the man. The blood had mostly clotted, and he still lay, sobbing. At the sight of the animal, certain that this was what had devoured his manhood, he scrabbled backwards, howling in fear, reopening his wound. The wolf-dog gazed at him with golden eyes and trotted after the two. A new story arose in the north, of a wolf, three-legged, the last of its kind, bent on revenge for the violence that humans had inflicted upon his race. For some decades later, men of the north pissed back to back or leaning on a tree, one hand cupping their balls, their eyes darting around instead of downwards at their pride and joy.

# 母ちゃん

## 「Kachan」

# 53

She would not hunt bear. Whenever she saw them, she greeted them as if they were family. They would rise in threat, their white crescent moon glowing against their black fur, and she would smile and softly speak as if to a brother or sister. She was mad, but no fool, and she knew just how close she could approach, laughing and talking, catching up on the news of the forest. Some bears would have none of this, and they would mock charge, something she would respect, retreating, her spear demanding respect in turn. Others found her an object of curiosity, and sometimes their meeting would go on and on. She sometimes grazed in the same berry bushes, only a couple of arms-length away.

With no old woman, no girl, no Kenko in her life, there was nothing to tether her mind in human ways, but she did not shatter as before. Her purpose shaped her; every evening, just after dusk, she spent several hours training, improvising everything they had taught her, and melded it into what she'd learned before as a hunter. Otherwise, she was mostly bear.

One late autumn evening, she awoke in a grove of *yaezakura*, mountain cherry trees, the leaves dark red. Assembling her matagi spear, she began taking leaves off a single limb of the tree, and then insects from the air. For the first time in ages, she thought clearly of her man. Perhaps it was company of the bears who brought him back, but she could remember all of him, all their days, not what it had been over these few years, a chaotic mélange where she could take no refuge in any memory without it suddenly ripping apart in blood and screams.

She remembered her man's story of his first hunt, where his father sent him with just a knife and a torch into the dark of a bear's cave, how he entered a boy and returned a matagi. Only a matagi could bring her child back, because that is from whom he was stolen. She was not sane, but she was herself, in a way she had not been since . . . then.

The wind blew bitter cold, biting through her clothes, but before she descended, she took out her two knives, and honed them on a rock.

# 54

Days passing into weeks, and weeks into winter. She saw no people, avoiding the few villages in the mountains, and perhaps this delayed her meeting, because the people in the north were in terror. The mountain demons seemed to be more active. More people had stories to tell, some bizarre, some terrible, but she heard none of that.

One night she heard a sound, a heartbreaking bawling of pain. Working her way through the forest, the snow thick on the ground, she entered a clearing and there was a bear, one of the largest she'd ever seen. It was tethered to several trees unable to move, each of its legs tied with thick plaited rope. In front of her, just out of reach, were her two cubs, yearlings: flayed. Their pelts were stripped from them, pulled almost off their paws and head, flapping and oozing blood as they struggled and died in the snow. They mewled and whimpered, and their mother struggled and bawled, unable to break free to them.

At the sight of her, the bear roared, foaming and gnashing her jaws. The Moongirl, her eyes filling with tears, quickly walked across the clearing and cut the cubs' throats, the mother bear thrashing, tearing its hide as she tried to rip free from the ropes.

Around the clearing, the woman saw footprints, large and small. She went close to the bear, right in the face of her, her raw smell filling the air. "I really don't know what to do, 'kachan. You have a right to hunt him, too, but I don't think you can do a thing. And you want to kill me too, don't you? All you know is that I stopped your babies' breath, and I look and smell the same as them . . ." (her voice caught), ". . .as him. I am going to set you free. If you would only do me the kindness of letting me be, then I will do what you could not. Let me be. Please."

She took her blade and quickly moved in front the bear.

Because of her immobility, the woman was able to get her blade underneath the coil and cut the loop off of one bloody leg. The moment the leg was free, the bear tried to whip around and savage her, but held still by three cords, she twisted and flipped onto her side. Before she could right herself, the woman cut the second coil.

It would be impossible to free her hind limbs the same way. The bear roared, struggling and ripping at the ropes. She did not seem to grasp that she could bite them, gnawing herself free, as a fox might. All she could do was lunge and whip from side-to-side, twisting backwards, trying desperately to sink her teeth in the woman.

The woman stilled her breath a moment, then walking in a crescent moon step, ever forward, from side to side, she slashed each rope in a figure-eight, she the central axis of her whirling blade. She slipped immediately to the side and behind a tree, and called, pleading, "Go to your babies, please!" But the bear had eyes only for her and charged, black blood splashing off from her limbs. They were among the trees now, the brush tight knit and the snow deep. The woman, moving and dodging, suddenly leapt towards the bear. Unlike most, however, the bear did not rise upwards to show her dominance. She just kept charging. The woman dropped low and sideways, her blade slipping under the muzzle of the bear, where it cut deeply into her throat. Just as the blade passed, with only the tip remaining, she momentarily pulsed her body, an internal convulsion, which drove the blade back in the direction it came, thrusting even deeper. She immediately reversed the convulsion again, as if a spring violently twisted deep within her, and the blade ripped a wide gash, severing her carotid artery.

It still took long minutes, the bear's roars changing to moans, ever charging, the woman slipping away, not wanting to cause her any more pain, giving her the honor of dying on her feet. Finally, the bear collapsed in the snow, the blood pumping from her neck. The woman went back to the clearing and picking up the cubs, pitiful little things, she brought them back to their mother. She smoothed their pelts back over their limbs, their heads and bodies, and laid them against her. The bear wrapped her bleeding head over her cubs, the bear died.

In the words her man had taught her, she prayed to them, mother and children, that their bravery, their strength and their love would fill her.

She arose and went back to the clearing, walking around, studying the footprints. From the dusting of snow, the tracks appeared only a few hours old, but no matter how hard she looked, she could find no footprints leading to or departing from the clearing. It was as if they had arrived by air.

Deep in the brush, however, opposite where this vile torment had been enacted, she found the footprints of her three-legged wolf-dog.

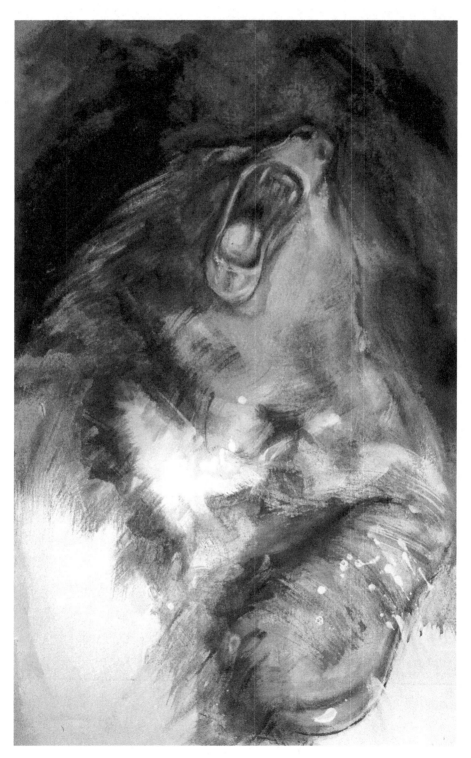

# 55

The sky was clouding over. She assembled her matagi knife and shaft once again into a spear, and followed the wolf-dog's trail. She could see where he paused, the prints deeper in the snow. In several places, he waited so long, unmoving, that his feet melted the snow, it refreezing to ice. His path was not a human path; he went under brambles, through narrow cracks between rocks, seemingly random meanders. On one occasion, she came to a dead-end—the tracks simply stopped and she realized that he had walked backwards in his own footsteps for nearly a mile.

As she tracked him, her senses remained alert. She smelled the air and listened for the slightest sound. She gazed around her, not only on the ground, but above as well, up in the trees. She moved so quietly that she almost stepped on a sleeping deer which, shocked by her sudden proximity, dashed away, his anthers brushing snow from the limbs around him. After he crashed through the brush, she stopped and stood without moving for five hundred feather-soft breaths, weapon ready.

Snow began to fall slowly, then harder, soft cottony flakes pouring from the sky. She began to move faster, worried that she would lose the trail. There on a thorn-bush was a tuft of hair. She was almost sure that it was him. But perhaps not. Could the trail be false?

In the faintest of voices, merely a breath with melody, she began to sing a song, a lullaby he'd surely heard many a night. Just as the trail vanished, a mound of snow broke open and he sprang upon her, too fast for her to react. She was helpless, the impact smashing her backwards, her spear arm deflected wide and helpless. Wolf-dog in her arms: heavy, squirming and licking her face frantically, but silent. He was trembling, but apart from the joy he so obviously felt, he was frightened, and he was enraged.

The snow was falling harder, yet dawn was reaching out, tendrils of light twining through the trees. She made a lean-to, and let the snow cover them. They huddled for warmth, but neither slept. She crouched, her spear at the ready, and he sat, ears forward, listening. The snow buried them, a blanket both chill and warm.

# 56

Buried alive. Particles of light exploded in miniscule novae through the snow, then winked out as the flakes piled deeper and deeper. It was worse than her years of wandering madness, worse than her embraces with woman-hating murderers, worse than her despair that dawn when Kenko crushed her hopes. She was back in a snow-cave, and she had no idea if he knew she was here, if he was stalking her in turn.

If they were stalking her.

Back she was, but not even half of her existed, for a soul is not enclosed within a sack of skin. A soul is the arc and compass of all that we love, and three parts of her soul were gone, a man and dog cut to tatters. And her boy? Where was he? What was he? That torture of her sister, the bear! Not only did the tracks tell their own tale, but no one, not even that demon thing could have trussed up a bear, not in that way. It took two.

She did not weep for what she was going to do. Her boy was truly gone. What was in the flesh of her child was not her son. She had two lives to take, not one.

The snow stopped some hours before dusk, and the wind blew hard for hours. The night fell bright and clear, the air tasting of pine and rock, and they broke through the glittering powder that blocked the entrance to the lean-to. The snow underfoot was crisp and dry, most of it piled in drifts against the trees. She'd kept her water bottle close to her skin, and she poured some in her hand, offering it to her wolf-dog, who lapped several hand-fuls and then stopped, gazing outwards, ears forward. She broke off some pieces of dried meat, gave half to him and ate the rest herself, softening it with sips of water. The months had pared her down. Her face was still round, but full of creases and lines, and her once glorious hair, haggard, iron grey.

Checking that her socketed knife was secured firmly on its spear shaft, and touching her other blade in her sash, she stood and said, "Time to hunt, yes?" Her wolf-dog stretched and quivered, shaking the shivers, her man used to say, and trotted to the northwest. He zigged and zagged, and circled back and forth. He'd find a line and dash off, return, then slightly change direction, and off he'd go again. She followed, breaking the pattern of her stride, touching the ground with each foot like a hand feeling the texture of skin, her body control so exquisite that she sensed brittle twigs, small pools of water skinned with ice and unstable ground, flowing like a shadow shed by clouds.

The woods were thick and dark. An occasional birch tree flamed like a white candle among the pines. Through the trees, one could gaze upwards to the river of night. Thankfully, no moon. Her eyes drank in shade: black and ash.

Half a night they stalked. The sky was just being to lighten, perhaps two hours before dawn. She had little time before she would once again have to hide from the burning flames of the day.

The trees broke and she stopped—several rows deep. In front of her was an expanse of river sand, with piles of boulders, cast down from a cliff that overlooked a small stream at its base. That slope rose gently at first, covered with massive cedars, then black rock suddenly seemed to thrust its way free above the trees. There, hundreds of feet up, was a small shape, a boy, her boy, edging his way up almost sheer granite towards the roost of a golden eagle. Since his violation of the woodcutter, he had continued to act on his own. The flying squirrel, a large-eyed velvety little thing, was long ago torn to shreds, and from then on, he seemed to hunt only that which was most wild, most beautifully free, most inaccessibly safe. The mother bear and her cubs were his, the Mantis merely playing a supporting role.

The eagle was aware of him, with his stone knife clenched between his teeth, and was nervously opening and closing her wings. Every move he made was done with finger and toe-tip.

178

One fraction of an inch off and he would die, but he ascended utterly at ease. The only way to kill the eagle was to climb over the ledge, right into her talons. He wanted to rip that feathered breast apart and eat her heart. He was twenty feet below, spread like a spider on the granite face.

She apprehended this in a single glance, and scanned the cliff and below for the Mantis. He was nowhere to be seen. Her wolf-dog, however, had bared his teeth and crouched down. He did not move. He made no sound. Suddenly he darted forward, seemingly attacking a boulder, a small round thing only a few dozen feet away. The rock exploded into grey tattered fabric, the smell of the grave blossoming from its folds. The wolf-dog lunged low, his teeth inches from the man-thing's groin. In a magnificent leap, the Mantis arched, one leg ascending, looping through the air and carrying the other in a three hundred sixty degree open spin. The wolf-dog did not hesitate, and sprung, from low to high like a wave breaking on the shore, following the Mantis skyward. His teeth closed on his thigh, but the Mantis ripped himself free, losing flesh, but not his artery, snapping his body in a convulsion like a snake grabbed by the tail. He dropped to the ground on his hands-and feet, belly low, and as the wolf-dog attacked again, circling behind to hamstring him, the Mantis bent himself double, shrimping himself head to foot. Grabbing the wolf-dog's crippled foreleg, the only thing in reach, he snapped it.

Simultaneous to the wolf-dog snapping his teeth at his face, however, he perceived a flash of movement from above, bright steel stabbing downwards. No time! He flung the wolf dog hard against the rocks, unconscious, hopefully dead, and rolled inwards away from the spear, towards the legs of his attacker, his obsidian fang already slashing, but all he met was air, as the legs twisted and spun out of the way. Again the blade descended, and his flesh parted, a gash across his back. Once again, his counter-stroke missed. His blood splattered the rocks as he rolled and twisted and somehow gained his feet, yanking his head to one side and down to avoid a thrust of the blade. He slithered his way behind a house-sized boulder, close to the stream.

Whatever had attacked him was the most astonishing being he had ever encountered. It was as fast as he. And the dog: just like that wolf-dog that was with the boy in the snow cave! Stepping around another rock, there she was. A rictus of astonishment cracked his face, his tongue licking the air across his cracked teeth. "So you live!" He cackled, remembering this, his only joke, the greatest suffering he'd ever inflicted. But once again, he felt fear. That sick feeling now returned, convulsing him inside out. He'd destroyed her, and here she was, a being transformed.

He pursed his lips and gave a short shrill whistle. The boy, high on the rock did not even glance backwards, merely reversed direction, and crept down the rock, a lizard-like slither.

She screamed, an eerie rasping cry that, starting low, somehow reached inside him, pulled him towards her, yes, even he, and then as the scream ascended, decibels rising with the pitch, he was frozen, just for a fraction of a second. He writhed sideways, dropped low and away, but his left arm trailed behind just a fraction, and she cut off his hand at the wrist. She continued the attack, slashing and stabbing, finally, finally, she was shedding his blood, but like the insect he was, in these brief moments, beyond his fear and his hate, he had coldly analyzed her, all of her. He juddered, moving three directions almost simultaneously. He took another slash on the neck, not deep, and a cut above the knee. When a limb is severed, the arteries close and lock down. But in the initial burst of blood, he managed to close his mouth over his wrist, and now he spat a mist, blacker than the night, blurring his form. He slipped within the cloud he'd made, and slashed her deeply across the belly.

Above them, unseen, the boy, still several hundred feet high, threw himself off the cliff, just like the momonga he'd torn to shreds. He spread his limbs and embraced the feathery top of a huge cedar tree fifty feet below him. Too slender for his weight, it broke and he fell, spinning, looping a hand here and a leg there, some branches breaking, some holding, slashing him, tearing him, slowing him down. He was on the ground running at the same moment his father slashed his prey, who was still screaming a rasping, bone-chilling cry.

The Mantis had not reached her vitals. She recoiled from the slash, covering her retreat while whirling her spear like a water-wheel, then raised the weapon, a straight line at eyebrow height, the blade pointed between his eyes. The Mantis was slowing, the loss of blood taking its toll, and she attacked, screaming again, a grating screech like talons scraped on slate, the knife-mounted spear shaft wavering in front of him, downwards, upwards, downwards, the coming attack unpredictable, and then, from behind, the boy leapt towards her, his blade stabbing at the small of her back.

She heard him and smelled him, the old woman's gifts fully hers, and she was perfect. She was faster than the owl that grabbed the mouse, faster than sparrow-wasps boiling from their nest, faster than the fire he set in the village, faster than the mother bear he so recently tortured. His blade a whisper away, she thrust the butt end of her weapon backwards, and it caught him right in the skull. The iron-capped wood struck with a crack, and he felt, unstrung, a rill of blood spilling from his head.

She used the recoil to power a thrust back at the Mantis, but he had moved as she did, a demonic mirror, and sweeping inwards, he thrust his knife back into his sash, and with his only hand, grabbed her spear shaft in the middle. She fought it, trying to channel his force into hers, but he took all she had and used it against her. His feet rooted in the sand, snapping his body like a doubled up whip, he wrenched her weapon away, throwing it across his body, and with his arm sweeping inward now, redrew his knife and slashed under her still upraised arm, severing the muscles of her triceps. One armed, he was more powerful than she with two, and now she was one-armed as well.

From the corner of her eye, she saw what she had struck. There was her baby, motionless on the ground, the blood slowly drip-ping down his face. She thought she had steeled herself for the worst, huddled in terror within a snow cave of her imagination. She was not prepared—not even after all those years of hope and agonized searching, of sacrifice beyond human measure. There was her boy, six years lost, wounded, perhaps dying at her own hand. She began screaming, screaming, screaming, and the Mantis stopped suddenly. He cocked his head to savor the sound, because this was exactly as she had screamed when he covered her with her husband's flesh. And there was his son, bloodied, to be sure, but he was coming to his senses. She couldn't see it, she was gazing at the Mantis now, she had eyes only for him, only the horror, but this time she was the horror. She'd killed her baby with her own hand, she screamed and screamed, while the boy gathered his senses, a hand on his knife. The Mantis grinned and waited for him to rip her to shreds, but just as the boy was coiling his limbs, a streak of golden-brown fur, three legs still fast enough, all eighty pounds of him smashed the boy down, and his jaws clamped round his throat, breaking skin, drawing blood, growling in rage. The boy made the slightest movement with his knife hand, and the wolf snarled deep in his throat and shook him—one fraction of power more and he'd tear out his throat.

Who was the boy to the wolf? He had followed the woman for six long years. This boy was only his pack mate, and as far as he was concerned, always beta to him. And now he is out of line. He's rolled him on his back and let him know his place, that's all wolves know anyway, what place they are in the family, and he will kill him if he moves, it's not his place to move, not against their mother. The boy is frozen, feeling the fangs, and his nose is filled with the smell of the dog, the smell of the dog, the smell of the dog, the teeth in his neck, he's felt those teeth before in mock fights, he knows that smell, he closes his eyes. Like heat lightning on the horizon, flickers of images flash behind his eyes, of climbing a tree and a woman following him, of wrestling with a dog, two dogs! And lullabies, of someone carrying him high above the forest floor, each memory rent and tattered as if by a giant clawed hand, memories of poisoned visions of hell in a womb, in the stinking embrace of his father. Not his father! There was a shaggy-headed bear of a man, hugging him, throwing him high, bending beside him showing him the track of a deer, laughing in the sun.

The cry of a mother bear, screaming, screaming, screaming, he hears screaming, a lullaby in an ice cave, screaming, a lullaby, screaming, screaming, a lullaby, a lullaby, and a tear, a single tear spills from his eye and he whispers, the first word he's said in a lifetime, "Kachan?"

All the Mantis sees is the wolf-dog at his son's throat, and he has no time for the pleasure he'd intended, of seeing her unstrung nerve by nerve, of even doing it himself, because he's still bleeding hard, he has little time left in this life and even more so, he has to go through her to get to the dog to save his son or the bloodline will die, and she's still screaming, her eyes blank and gone, back in the ice cave covered in flesh and slashed to ribbons, and he moves, a dragonfly dart, and stabs her right in the throat . . . . but just as the tip scores her neck, she, screaming still, drops boneless underneath his blade, then explodes, her scream incandescent, a banshee wail of rage, and she rams Kenko's knife beneath his ribs into his heart. She is still screaming, but with only one arm, she cannot push him away, and collapsing forwards, he stabs her in the back, severing her spine. They fall, wrapped within each other.

The boy has put his arms around the wolf-dog, simply holding him, and he opens his fangs and licks the blood from the boy's face. He rolls to his side and the wolf-dog releases him, whips around, snarling, towards the Mantis.

The boy crawls forward, and pulls the body of him away from the body of her. His rags soaked in blood, he lies, a jumble of bone and flesh, an ill-smelling heap.

The boy's mind is chaos, swathes of memory, one life of love, one life of terror, overlapping, twining, braiding, each ripping the other to shreds. She is laying face down, the stone knife between her shoulder blades. He pulls it free. She is paralyzed, and she is bleeding her life out onto the rocks. He rolls her on her back.

# Face of the moon!

He sits gazing at her face, his eyes luminous and blank. With her dying breaths, she tells him a story of a crab that marched up a mountain to get her revenge on a monkey that killed her mother, and her allies: the mortar, the horseapple, the pestle, the wasp, and the egg and what they did, the words mere puffs of air, and his eyes are luminous and blank, and she dies.

# 57

Two eagle soar overhead. Two bodies lie below. A boy with luminous eyes. The world oscillates, shifting from vision—a cliff, a river, trees and snow—to fractal spirals, shimmering clouds, much as his mother, light-blind, once saw.

He sits rocking. A refrain mumbles and buzzes from his lips: *Kani-don. Kani-don. Doko iku no? Saru no bamba e, adauchi ni . . .* Mrs. Crab. Mrs. Crab. Where are you going? I'm going to the monkey's place to take my revenge. *Kani-don. Kani-don. Doko iku no?*

Silent
then again.
And again.

And again.

Silent.
And again.

A three-legged wolf-dog leans upon him, nudges his arm up and over his back. His already crippled leg is broken again, but no whimpers from him. He shoves his muzzle under the boy's chin, licks his face, gusts breath in his face. The boy rocks and hums.

# 58

Days pass. The snow flurries and swirls. The boy shivers and hums. The wolf-dog comes-and-goes with his rocking gait, wounded limb close to his chest, muzzle wet with blood from a kill. The bodies, white and grey and blue, drift with snow. One body reeks, a charnel smell. The boy idly picks up an obsidian knife, slices the remaining hand off the corpse and throws it aside.

A keening cry, the eagle, she swoops, snatches the hand and brings it to her nest. The boy's eyes, dark glowing pools, follow her flight up the rocks he so recently climbed, murder in his limbs.

He turn towards the corpse and a momentary snarl twists his face, fear and rage and hate, then it returns to blank, his eyes dark galaxies, snow and starlight.

He suddenly stands, his limbs creaking with cold. Grabbing one ankle, casually, effortlessly, the little boy drags the corpse over river rocks and driftwood, as easily as you or I might pull a scarf. At the base of the cliff, he strips it of its stinking rags, cuts them into ribbons, frays the ribbons into single threads and lets them drift away like spider webs. Then, squatting, he butchers the corpse and leaves the meat and bones into a pile, cut into pieces no bigger than his own hand. The eagles swirl overhead, keening, eying the bounty.

He reserves two things: fingers and head. He flenses the face, cracks open the skull, meat and brain added to the pile. The skull, he crushes to powder, the fingers, he crushes to paste, and onto the pile they go. All that's left is the eyes, which he holds in the palm of his hand. They stare at him as they've done for years, without love, hope or care. He gazes back, his eyes luminous and blank.

He goes to the riverbank, begins to cast them into the water, then stops, returns, begins to put them on the pile of meat, eagles keening above, then stops.

He turns again, he places them on a flat stone at the river's edge, and with another rock, grinds them into paste, into rock, into molecules, they mix with the falling snow, and he grinds some more, for a day he grinds these eyes, half the rock is ground away, the melted snow, the rock, washes into the stream, that awful gaze, that soul eating stare, his father's eyes, washed away.

# 59

His luminous eyes, they gaze into fractal spirals, he sits rocking beside his mother's body, a refrain mumbling and buzzing from his lips: *Kani-don. Kani-don. Doko iku no? Saru no bamba e, adauchi ni* . . . Silence, then again. A three-legged wolf dog leans upon him, nudges his arm up and over his back. His already crippled leg is broken again, no whimpers from him. He shoves his muzzle under his chin, licks his face, gusts breaths in his face. The boy rocks and hums.

His mother's eyes stare upwards into the sky, into the falling snow.

He reaches out to touch her, he pulls back, he reaches out, he reaches out, he cannot touch her, he cannot cut her, life feeds life, death feeds life, but the eagles shall not have her.

The bears shall not have her.

The worms shall not have her.

He piles driftwood. He places her on the driftwood, it is so hard to touch her, this boy who has burned villages, burned men and women and babies. The wolf-dog circles, whimpers, then howls. He lights the fire, red-flower blooming amidst the snow.

She burns, she burns, he adds more wood, she burns, she's smoke, she's gone. She is the sky.

His eyes gaze upwards, luminous and blank. She gazes back at him, stars.

# 60

They wander far from humanity. When he is near, the craving makes him shake: Burn it! Burn them! Cut them!

The boy hunts. He kills, but he more than kills. Animal by animal, he gazes into their pain-ripped eyes, and still sees his mother, sees his father, sees quick joy and fierce love, sees what he is not. He has to eat and so he does, but mostly, overwhelmed by lust to tear and rend, he destroys the quick and alive.

When the wolf-dog is near, the urge is overwhelming, he shakes with it.

The wolf-dog knows none of this. He kills to eat, not to torment, and as far as he is concerned, the boy wastes time, chasing nightingales and sparrow-wasps, and then wastes more, reducing them nerve by nerve to incandescent pain. The boy makes no sense, and nonsense only makes hunger.

He gambols around the boy, chews lightly on his leg, tugging him, cajoling him to go on the hunt. He licks his face, he whines, and the boy looks in his eyes, untamed and alive, golden-brown, the wolf-dog's eyes glow. Without thought, the boy lashes out with his blade and slashes his pack-mate, splitting one ear to the skull. He yelps, then snaps with a snarl, teeth a whisper from the boy's face. The boy sways back like an adder, then leaps forward, grabs his ruff and stabs, the blade plunging towards the wolf-dog's heart.

The wolf-dog shimmies like quicksilver poured over rock, and the blade misses, rips through flesh and scores a rib, he cries in anguish, the wolf-dog cries, he tears himself out of his grasp and cowers back to the edge of the clearing. His eyes blank and luminous, the boy stoops and picks up a stone. The wolf-dog knows what comes next, he's gone, a granite wasp humming into where he was.

Boy alone. Wandering. The world oscillates, shifting from vision—a cliff, a river, trees and snow—to fractal spirals, shimmering clouds.

# 61

There's still ice on the ground, but spring's plum trees are now in bloom, deep pink, their creamy scent wafting over piles of snow drift. She's walking amongst the trees singing, she's been helping her mother all day, and now she follows a spinning whirligig her father made, as if it wafts her along by the tips of her fingers, pulling her deeper into the trees.

Smashed down, her lips crushed into the gritty snow, mouth bleeding. Rolled over. A boy with luminous eyes stares into hers. A stone knife at her throat, he slowly cuts, blood spilling. He smells the plum blossoms, he smells her hair, he smells her breath. Alive, she's alive. Her eyes are alive. Not flat, not dead, they are full of tears. She whimpers. She's quick and changeable. She cannot be controlled, she cannot be known, not while alive. She needs to be dead. He cuts deeper.

He stops. His mother's eyes were alive. His were dead. He made others like himself. Only eyes can cause pain. He cannot look. He cannot cut.


He's gone.


She told her father she thought he was a *tengu*, though his nose was short and he didn't have a beak or feathers.


Her father kept her close to home for a long time.


She was never scared of anything again. She told her mother that death looked her in the eyes and he could not kill her. She later married a man who kissed the scar on her neck before he kissed her lips.

# 62

He stops killing those with warm bodies, then things with feathers, then things with scales. No matter how alien, they still have eyes.

Alone, the boy wanders through forested hills, then up a stony path to a small shrine for mountain ascetics. At its side is a egg-shaped boulder, with a red apron round its middle, two holes bored for eyes and two for nostrils, and a faint smile scratched below.

The boy squats down and stares into its eyes. The rock stares back at him.

# 63

A small stream flows out of the rocks, round the back of the shrine. He sips cool water, bending until his lips touch the surface, and quietly draws it into his mouth. Then he returns to the rock. Already half-starved, the boy stares and the rock, smiling, stares back.

Weeks pass. He has wasted away, bones and skin. The clouds lower and there is a fog around the mountain top. The boy sits unmoving, staring, and the fog thickens and the rock is gone. No one is gazing back at him.

He reaches out his hands and frantically tries to brush the fog from the air, but it flows on, thick and indifferent. With his obsidian blade, he slashes once and again, but he cannot cut clouds. The blade strikes the stone and shatters, shards and needles scoring his face, the blood runs down in streams.

He cannot see the stars where the smoke of his mother's body returned, he cannot see the rock.

The wet cold settles into his bones. Lurching forward, his head cracks on the rock he cannot see. He wraps his arms around it. No arms hold him in return.

He desperately clings to the rock. The fog thins and he stares into holes that pass for eyes. The rock smiles blankly.

He suddenly shrieks, he suddenly cries. He cries an eagle's keen that spirals up and up and up, then breaks and plunges, convulses, turns him inside out. He clings desperately to the rock, but no arms hold him back, he cries, a baby on a rubbish heap, a boy in a stinking pit poisoned with horror and thorn-apple, a boy whose mother is smoke and stars, a boy whose fathers are scraps of meat, he sobs so deeply he cannot breathe, his heart is pounding no air,

no breath, no air,
surrounded by air, by life

none for him

no breath, no air

he clings to the rock for life it will not give, it smiles blank, its eyes mere holes

And a warm fury head rounds the rock, stares deeply into his eyes. One ear split and ragged torn, the wolf-dog stares, the boy stares back, his eyes spilling tears, the boy's eyes soft and brown, and the boy's sob breaks and he gasps and
the wolf-dog pries his head between rock and arms,

forces his way in the circle of the boy's arms,

huffs his breath into the boy,

the little sobbing boy stares into his eyes,

all life.

# 螳螂

「mantis」

# 64

A mountain village. A spring night, the stars in the sky, the crickets chirping, and bats fluttering: a beautiful night. And grunting, yelling, and things breaking. A woman crying in pain. "You fucking cunt." Sound of a blow. A beautiful night. The crickets chirping, a woman weeping, a baby screaming that rasping cry for which there is no comfort, the people of the neighboring hovels shaking their heads in disgust. He'll kill her one day, that one: her or the kid.

The man stumbles out, reeking of drink. There is a cloud of fireflies around the well, and he stops, for a moment entranced. From among the glowing green sparks steps a wolf and a boy, a man, a wrinkled old geezer bent and seemingly frail, for this story happens again and again, in different places, in different times. His eyes are luminous and blank. He moves faster than thought. He kills no one, but hurts them in ways so profound that they cannot even begin to scream, all in an instant an eternity long, and then, he visits them every so often, sometimes day-after-day, sometimes not for years, their wives and children asleep beside them. They wake with him sipping their breath, his eyes luminous and blank, and he whispers, "No." They nod, shivering in fear and remembered pain. He closes their eyes with a hand as hard and calloused as horn. He's gone.

And the story goes that once there was a demon, maybe there were two, no one knows for sure, and through the blessings of Kannon, the goddess of mercy, that monster who took the lives of children and mothers became their guardian, became a living incarnation of the bodhisattva Jizo, and for decades, men of the north not only clutched their balls in fear of the wolf demon, but they also thought twice before they struck their wives or children, because one never knew who might be watching.

To my mother, Evelyn Amdur
(October 28th, 1921 – February 29th, 2004).

You would have come for me.

# About the Author

Ellis Amdur went to Japan at the age of twenty-three. He lived there thirteen years, studying classical Japanese martial arts. He's now trained in such arts for fifty years. He is a recognized expert in classical and modern Japanese martial traditions, and has authored three iconoclastic books on this subject.

Upon his return to America, he began working in the field of crisis intervention. He has authored eighteen profession-specific books in this area, some written with subject-matter-expert co-authors concerning tactical communication with seriously mentally ill individuals and verbal de-escalation of aggression.

He has collaborated with authors Neal Stephenson, Mark Teppo, Charles Mann and artist Robert Sammelin in the graphic novel series, Cimarronin: A Samurai in New Spain.

All of his work can be found at www.edgeworkbooks.com.

This is his first novel.